I0545736

Oak

PG Forte

Copyright © 2018 PG Forte
Chapultepec Press
ISBN: 978-1-880370-27-8
Editor: Maryam Salim
Cover artist: PG Forte

All rights reserved. Without limiting the rights under copyright reserved above, no part of this publication may be reproduced, stored in or introduced into a retrieval system, or transmitted, in any form, or by any means (electronic, mechanical, photocopying, recording or otherwise) without the prior written permission of both the copyright owner and the above publisher of this book.

This is a work of fiction. Names, characters, places, brands, media, and incidents are either the product of the author's imagination or are used fictitiously. The author acknowledges the trademarked status and trademark owners of various products referenced in this work of fiction, which have been used without permission. The publication/use of these trademarks is not authorized, associated with, or sponsored by the trademark owners.

Dedication

In memory of my mother, who taught me about trees.

And for Dawn, who loves them as much as I do.

Chapter One

*"The Oak King and the Holly King doth rule the forest green,
One bright and fair as a summer's morn, one dark as a
winter's e'en.
Twice in each year the two must meet to do battle for the
throne,
And one shall remain in the goddess's arms, while the other
shall rule alone."*

*Ireland
December 1895
One night before the solstice*

"Who is it you're thinkin' of tonight? Is it he?"

At the sound of her husband's voice, Aine's thoughts scattered like a flock of birds flushed out of hiding. She paused in the act of brushing her hair and met his gaze in the mirror above her dressing table. "What an odd question. Why do you ask?"

"There's a dreamy look upon your face."

"Is there?"

"Aye, lass, there is."

Aine bit back a sigh. There was a look on Fionn's face, too, and it was anything *but* dreamy. Brooding and unhappy, it caused an ache in Aine's heart. For all that he'd wronged her by tricking her into this marriage—keeping the truth of his nature a secret until after they'd wed—Aine still loved him. For an instant, she even considered denying his accusation, but what good would that do? The guilty blush heating her cheeks had surely given her away by now.

Nor would she insult them both by asking Fionn who he

meant. She knew of only one man who could put so bitter a tone in Fionn's voice, only one man to whom he could possibly be referring. Kieran. Fionn's other half. His opposite. And Aine's…

Ah, well now, that was the question, wasn't it? What *was* Kieran to her?

He wasn't family, despite what her neighbors had been told or might choose to believe. Though he and Fionn were as intimately connected as twins, their lives forever entwined, the two men were definitely *not* brothers. He wasn't Aine's lover either, no matter how much she might desire him, or how much Fionn might fear that was the case. In fact, now that she'd thought on it, she *did* know what Kieran was to her. He was a *geis*—a curse. He was a burden she'd taken on, all-unknowing, when she'd married Fionn. A burden she must live with for six months out of every year.

Very soon, Kieran would be by her side once again with those eyes that seemed to gaze straight into her soul, with that smile that could tempt even the most virtuous of angels into sinning, and that voice that…well, even thinking about it now caused her heart to race and her chest to ache with longing.

Strong but wounded, charming yet aloof, handsome, tormented, and just the slightest bit wicked—had there ever been a more enticing combination in a man? And that was *before* she'd learned of Kieran's secret, a secret he'd hidden so well, and buried so deeply within him, she wasn't certain he knew it himself. He was in love with her husband.

Did their mutual love for Fionn make for a bond between herself and Kieran, or did it put them at odds with one another? Aine wasn't sure which was the case. Either way, it was reason enough for her to distrust him, or at the very least, to distrust her feelings toward him.

And, either way, she'd soon be welcoming him back into her home, as she had last year, and would continue to do every year to come. Once again they'd be sleeping under the same roof, sharing their meals and their thoughts, keeping each other company through the long winter nights and soft spring days while Fionn was away.

In truth, the prospect excited her far more than it should.

Realizing the direction her thoughts had taken, Aine all but rolled her eyes. She could hardly say any of *that* to her husband! "The solstice is nigh upon us, my love," she said instead. "'Twould be wondrous strange were I *not* to be thinking of him at such a time. Would it not?"

"Aye," Fionn replied in grudging tones. "It would at that."

Aine felt her gaze soften as she looked upon her husband. He was so handsome, so serious, so concerned. He seemed larger than life—which, in a way, she supposed he was—and completely out of place in their tidy little bedroom.

Even in the depths of winter, Fionn's skin retained the same rosy flush it had worn when first they'd met, as though he spent every day standing outside in the hot sun. He radiated warmth, vitality, and strength—the very picture of every lush, summer day that had ever dawned, all rolled into one. And all hers to enjoy.

The thought sent a delicious thrill rushing through her, as it did each time she remembered it. Tonight, however, it also brought a renewed sense of urgency. For with Kieran's arrival, Fionn would once again be forced to leave her.

Six long months would pass before they would see each other again, and all she'd have to carry her through until summer would be the memory of these days together. She ached to once more feel his body on hers—now, while she still had the chance. She yearned for those strong arms to wrap around her and hold her close, for those sure, masterful hands to caress her skin and bring her to ecstasy over and over again. The time left to them grew so short.

"'Tis you I married," she said, as she resumed the task of dragging her brush through her long red hair. "If you remember nothing else, Fionn, I bid you remember that. 'Tis *you* who are my husband."

"Aye. That I am." A satisfied smile curved Fionn's lips. His eyes lit up with a fierce, possessive gleam. Pulling back the bedcovers, he beckoned to her. "Now come here to me, wife, and let me remind you of that fact."

Those words, that smile, that devilish gleam—the fact that he refused to wear any form of nightclothes, no matter how cool the night—were all the inducement Aine needed. His muscles gleamed in the candlelight, and even the shadows teased her with thoughts of what they concealed. A tide of need rushed through her, bringing the blood flooding into her cheeks once again, turning her knees weak. Her nipples hardened into two tight buds that pushed against the fabric of her nightgown, rubbing against the rough weave with every breath she took, every move she made. Inside and out, she was awash with sensation. He hadn't so much as touched her yet, and still warmth pooled in her belly.

Abandoning her brush, she blew out her candles, then rose to her feet. Starlight lit her way as she crossed the room—with far more speed than grace, mostly due to the cold wooden floor beneath her feet. She slid between the sheets Fionn had been warming for her and allowed him to pull her down to lie beneath him. Her heart racing with excitement, she could not help but be reminded of the first time he'd made love to her, the first kiss they'd shared, that first morning they'd met...

She still could scarce believe how quickly she'd surrendered to him. The giddy heat that had flowed through her that day had all but demanded it.

She caged his face in her hands and smiled down at him teasingly, so besotted she could think of nothing else but getting naked with him, of putting his cock inside her and riding him hard. It didn't even matter where they were—right there in her parlor, in the middle of the day with the curtains pulled back and the windows open to the warm summer breeze, so that anyone riding by might hear them or that anyone who stopped to investigate would surely see them.

None of it mattered. She wanted him. No. She needed him. Right there, right then.

His hands tightened on her waist. She lowered her head and pressed her lips to his, and the heat that blazed between them incinerated all that was left of her doubts. His taste, earthy, sweet, and smoky, tantalized her. She was certain she'd never tire of the taste of him, never have enough...

"You're shivering," Fionn said now as he gazed down upon her. He skimmed his hand up and down her arm. A worried frown creased his brow. "Are you cold, my love?"

Aine shook her head as she snuggled closer, too desperate to offer protest. It was her need for him that was making her shiver. If there was any benefit to be derived from the strange circumstances that governed their lives, it was this: they could never take this joining of their bodies for granted. It would never grow dull or rote, never get old. Much like Fionn himself, she supposed, but that thought was unwelcome, so she pushed it aside.

Fionn's hand slid through her hair to grip the back of her head, and Aine moaned with pleasure. Once again, she reached for him. Their lips met in an eager, openmouthed kiss. His tongue swept inside, swamping her senses and driving all other thoughts from her head. There it was again, the elusive flavor that was purely Fionn.

When she slipped a hand between them and found his cock, Fionn groaned in response. He was ready for her, but that was hardly a surprise. He was almost always ready for her, it seemed. As Aine slid her hand teasingly up and down the length of him, Fionn used the fingers of his free hand to tease her breasts. He pinched a nipple, and she arched into him. Her sex pulsed demandingly, and she squirmed, needy, hungry, wanting...something. Wanting... Yes. Wanting *more.*

Guilt teased at her conscience. Perhaps it was wrong of her to yearn for something else tonight, to ache for anything more than what she had right here. But right or wrong, 'twas how she felt. Tonight, she could only be fully satisfied with two sets of hands on her body, touching her everywhere. Two mouths. Two tongues. Two cocks. Two men... Perhaps the idea should have shocked her—and perhaps it had, the first few times she'd thought it. But that had been so many months ago, she could hardly recall it. By now, she'd grown so very accustomed to the notion that it seemed quite natural—not a new thought at all, but a desire she'd been born with.

It was not that she was unhappy with Fionn—never that. Nor was it something she felt the need for all the time. But every so often she wanted to have them both. And not just individually, one man at a time, which would have been almost understandable given her peculiar circumstances. Oh no, she wanted more even than that. She wanted the two of them together, both at once.

The thought, so deliciously wicked, heated her blood to a fever pitch as images unfurled once more in her head, as she pictured the two handsome, virile, thoroughly engrossing men pleasuring her and, yes, pleasuring each other as well. The three of them together, completing each other.

That was just one of the lessons she'd learned from Kieran last year, the fact that it was indeed possible to love two men at once. But was that something that Fionn could ever accept?

On the face of it, it seemed impossible. Why, as far as she could tell, the two men could barely speak a civil word to one another. Then too, the amount of time they actually had to spend together was so short—just a single night here, a handful of days there. How was she to bring about the desired result?

It wasn't for her sake alone that she wanted it either, but for theirs as well. She'd read their hearts these past twelve months. She'd uncovered their secrets, buried and long denied. Their lives were filled with so much unnecessary loneliness. How could she not even try and heal that?

Only one thing was certain. These days and nights surrounding the winter solstice were the most magical of the year. Ruled in part by the dangerously wicked Lord of Misrule, they were also the darkest and most illicit. If ever there was a time to make such a wish, or to have it granted, it was surely now.

FIONN TIGHTENED ONE hand in his wife's hair, using just enough pressure to hold her in place so he might plunder her mouth at will. Meanwhile, he shifted his other hand back and forth, first at one breast, then the other, visiting sweet torment on each tender tip. Tugging, twisting, teasing her until she tore her mouth away from his with a shattered gasp and a helpless cry. "Enough, Fionn, please. I need you inside me now."

"Nay, my love. 'Tis not nearly enough." In truth, he did not think he could *ever* have enough of her. He could make love to her for days on end, and it would still not satisfy him. Not that he had days on end at this point. The knowledge of how little time was left to them blew through him like a cold north wind. It beat relentlessly at his senses. *Never enough, never enough, never enough time.* "Spread your legs for me now, my darling," he ordered as he slid down her body, impatiently shoving her gown out of his way. "Let me pleasure you."

Aine whimpered in anticipation as she complied with his request, eagerly opening herself to him. Fionn settled himself between her thighs, breathing in her fragrance as he did, so spicy and warm in the cool night air, so endlessly enticing. Nearly overcome by the desire to brand her with his touch, he began to press soft kisses along the tender skin of her thighs.

Aine wiggled impatiently. "Fionn, please!"

Fionn couldn't help but smile. "Oh I will please you, my love, never fear. But you must allow me to do so at my own pace. Some things should not be rushed."

He slid his hands beneath her hips and lifted her slightly, then used his thumbs to spread her folds, noting how slick they were already, how plump and swollen. Using the flat of his tongue, he licked up the length of her sex. He flicked the tight bud of her clit several times, circled the hood with his tongue, then flicked some more. When Aine's hips began to buck, he tightened his grip to hold her still and slowed his already languorous pace.

"Fionn!" Aine groaned, hands clenching in the sheets. "Now. I beg you!"

Chuckling, Fionn changed tactics. He speared his tongue inside her, loving both the salty-sweet taste of her juices and the strangled sound of her voice as she chanted his name. When he decided she'd had enough teasing, he replaced his tongue with his fingers, then resumed his attack on her clit. He bent his head to take it in his mouth, sucking and licking in time with his thrusts until her inner walls closed around his hand and her whole body convulsed as she came.

Before she was finished, he surged on top of her. He was impatient for his own release and eager for the feel of her arms and legs as they wrapped around him and held him tight, for the sweet warmth of her pussy as it clenched his cock.

"Fionn," she whispered again as her nails bit into his shoulders. "*A ghrá geal.*"

And it seemed to Fionn that her words were both a prayer and a promise. And he spilled inside her wishing that it could always be so, that he could always be to her what he was tonight—*the bright love of her life.*

Afterward, Aine sighed contentedly as she settled into his arms. The sleepy silence should have been peaceful. Instead it felt anxious, restless, and edgy. A heavy frost lay upon Fionn's heart, and he could not quiet his troubled thoughts. All too soon he would be gone, and Kieran would take his place. Oh, not in Aine's bed, perhaps, nor even in her heart—at least not right away. No, it would not be tonight or possibly not even this next year, but eventually...

Surely it was bound to happen. Married or not, it seemed it was only a matter of time before he lost her. For why should she not give herself to whomever she chose? And, that being so, why should she not want the more worthy of them to be her consort?

Fionn tightened his grip on Aine's shoulders. Yes, she was still his tonight, and he would fight to keep her for as long as possible, but his chances seemed bleak. How much longer could he hope to prevail? He sighed heavily.

At the sound, Aine lifted her head to look at him. "What is it that troubles you, my love? Whatever it is, I'm certain it cannot be so bad as your sighs would make it seem. Surely there can be no more deep, dark secrets you've neglected to share with me?"

"No, 'tis nothing like that." Fionn brushed the hair back from her face and gazed back at her, pensively. "I've been thinking about something you said earlier. And while 'tis true it's me you married, still I cannot help but wonder whether that would have been the case were you to have met *him* first."

Aine sighed. "Are you asking if I would have married Kieran instead? Ah, love, how am I to answer such a question? In truth, I do not know. I will tell you this, however. I would change nothing about the past. It's glad I am that I met you when I did, for you are indeed *a cuislĕ mo chroi*, the pulse of my heart. And strange though this life may be, and however uncertain our future, I do believe I would not have had it any other way."

Chapter Two

Fifty-seven years earlier
June 1837
At the time of the summer solstice

The Holly King was not happy. Kieran Mac Cuilenn, Lord of Misrule and Ruler of the Waning Year, had been awake since before the dawn, intent on making the most of every last minute of freedom before his six-month reign began. He was also eager to be reunited with his lover, if only for a few short hours. But the day was swiftly passing, and the Oak King had yet to make an appearance. This made the third time since sunrise that Kieran had climbed to the top of this lonely hill to stand beside the Oak King's tree, to lay a hand against the oak's rough bark and whisper words of encouragement. But, just like the last two times, his pleas went unanswered. Naught but the faintest of pulses emanated from within the massive trunk, letting him know that his friend and lover continued to slumber.

"Damn you, Rory," Kieran grumbled as worry and disappointment ate away at his temper. "What ails you? Why won't you wake up?" He struck the tree with his fist, feeling more like a petulant child than a mature *dru* just settling into midlife.

He sighed in exasperation. Every summer it grew harder to coax the older tree spirit from his tree. At this pace, it would not be long before the only time they saw each other was at the winter solstice, which was under Kieran's control. If that was to be the way of it, he was half-tempted to play the same sort of game this next December.

Why should he not pay Rory back in kind for worrying him so? But he knew he would never carry through with the threat. Their time together was already so short; anything less was unacceptable. All the same, however, *something* would have to be done. Kieran had been as patient as he knew how.

The time had come for action.

"I'll be back soon, you old goat," Kieran promised, dealing the heavy trunk another sharp blow. "And, when I return, I *will* have you out of there if I have to set fire to your roots to do so." Then he turned and headed back down the hill, a foggy idea already beginning to take shape.

He'd tried soft words and sweet enticements—they hadn't worked—and Kieran was no longer in the mood for gentle coaxing. He would find another way to rouse Rory and draw him forth. All he needed was the proper goad, something to ignite the Oak King's passion and force him from slumber. But what?

He'd gone no distance at all before the exact thing he needed appeared to him in the person of a handsome young dru lurking in the shadows of the trees adjacent to the path Kieran trod.

Kieran's footsteps slowed. The lad was vaguely familiar, though Kieran did not know him by name. Something about the self-conscious expression on the youth's face, the flush on his cheeks, the awkward way he dived for the shelter of the trees as though attempting to conceal himself, caught Kieran's attention. He stopped in his tracks and fixed the lad with a piercing gaze. "You, there. Come out here at once and tell me what you are doing."

The young man flushed even harder. "Why, n-nothing, sire. I mean, Y-your Majesty." Taking a deep breath, he squared his shoulders, then stepped boldly onto the path. "I was just... I'd hoped..." Abruptly the lad dropped to his knees and bowed his head. "I wanted to wish you a H-happy Solstice, m-my liege."

"Happy?" Kieran repeated the word thoughtfully. He did not consider either of the solstices to be joyful occasions. Once he might have done so, he supposed, but they'd long since become the dreariest of days, forever associated with sacrifice and loss.

"Aye, Your Majesty. And also...to wish you well as your reign commences." He paused, tongue darting nervously out to wet his lips, then continued in a rush. "I know you are always with us, my liege, whether we see you or no. But the world will seem a bleaker place until you return again to grace us with your presence."

"I see." Kieran felt a rush of attraction such as he could not remember feeling in a very long time. It was followed almost immediately, however, by one of regret. What a shame they had not crossed paths earlier in the year. As it was, he now had no time to pursue anything with… "Stand up, my boy. And, tell me, what is your name?"

"F-fionn, m-my liege," he said rising slowly to his feet. "Fionn O'Dair."

Fionn. Kieran repeated the name silently. He would really have to try and remember that. "Well, I thank you, Fionn, for your well wishes." The boy was delightful, bright as a summer morn—an oak, obviously—and, perhaps because of that, Kieran was suddenly reminded, most forcefully, of Rory.

It was then that the half-realized ideas in Kieran's head coalesced into a plan. What better way to gain the Oak King's attention than to flaunt a new lover in front of him, to make love to this lad right in the shade of Rory's branches? Why, nothing could be more perfect! He could indulge in a harmless flirtation with Fionn and roust Rory from his bed at the same time.

Knowing Rory as he did, Kieran was certain the oak would waste no time in making Kieran pay for his insolence. He'd be wont to take his wayward lover hard and fast—very much in the same manner as Kieran planned on taking Fionn, if he were willing. The thought only added to Kieran's excitement.

A smile overspread Kieran's face. "I wonder, young Fionn, how sincere are you in wishing me happy? For, if you're willing, I can think of a way in which you might assist me in making this solstice a very happy one indeed."

* * * *

The world was not what it once was. Of that Rory Tighearnach, high king of the drus—the tree spirits of *Éire*—was certain. Why, he had only to look around him to see the proof of that! His home grove was naught but a memory now. All of his family, stately creatures, tall and proud, trees that had once clustered about him, that had sheltered him from wind and rain when he was but a seedling, were long gone. Even the deer and the squirrels that had once lingered in their shade, or browsed upon the abundance of acorns and nuts the trees let fall, had deserted him. He alone remained now, surrounded by gorse and furze and heather, with only a handful of birds—who still returned, year after year, to make their nests in his branches—for company.

Were he a simple dru, like others of his kind, he would have long since moved on. For contrary to what the legends claim, tree spirits are not solitary by nature, nor must they remain always where their trees are rooted. But Rory's life was no longer his own. It was ages ago that he was proclaimed Oak King, Lord of the Forest, Protector of the Greenworld, Ruler of the Waxing Year. And with that honor had come the responsibilities that kept him bound here.

For six months—midwinter to midsummer—Rory was held in a kind of stasis, unable to take shape or venture forth. That was just his body, of course, but his mind was also not his own. Though not similarly constrained to remain in one place, it was almost completely subsumed by the Forestmind. His awareness flowed outward, through a wide and varied network of root and branch, rhizome and filament. Working its way through lichen and algae, through seaweed and moss, it circled the globe. It was everywhere at once, cognizant of all that transpired within the entirety of the Greenworld.

It *was* an honor to have been chosen for so exalted a purpose. And there was, undeniably, a certain amount of bliss to be had in his yearly melding with a will so much greater than his own. But it was a burden also. Some years, he'd been scarcely able to wait for the summer solstice to arrive. He'd been so eager to be released from his service—freed to

be just himself once again—that he'd fair burst from his tree
the first moment he was able.

More and more often, however, he'd begun to find
himself reluctant to return to regular consciousness. The
magic needed to extricate himself from his tree seemed more
elusive than in years past. The Greenworld continued to pull
at his soul in a way it had not done before. He could feel it
calling him, urging him to stay submersed in its depths, to
lose himself within it. Perhaps to lose himself permanently.

Today, for example, though the morning had fled—and
most of the afternoon as well—he had yet to make the
slightest effort to free himself. He could not recall a single
reason why he should. Did the noonday sun not feel pleasant
as it caressed his leaves? Was not the warm breeze that
stirred amid his topmost branches a delight to experience?
Why not tarry a while longer, right where he was, dreaming
of days gone by? Why force himself to face the reality of a
world grown bleak and dismal?

The sound of laughter filtered into his thoughts, such a
gentle, rousing sound. Rory smiled when its source was
revealed. Two drus were at play upon his hill, pursuing each
other through the brush—naked and unafraid. As well they
might be. For even if there had been humans present, they
would not be seen. Human senses could not pierce the magic
veil that had been erected to keep the two species separated.

But ah, their laughter took him back, it did. Once upon a
time he too had played such games. It warmed his heart to
realize there was still some joy left in the world. His heart
heated even more when he recognized one of the two men.
Kieran Mac Cuilenn, the Holly King, he who ruled over the
Waning Year.

The other dru was as yet unknown to him. Rory studied
the newcomer with some interest. He was tall, though still
somewhat gangly, with a curly mop of copper-colored hair
bleached gold in places by the sun. Judging by his coloration
and his build, Rory could tell he was an oak, but a very
young one, little more than a stripling.

Kieran led his playmate to the very foot of Rory's tree. There the chase ended. Kieran turned and fixed his pursuer with a heated gaze—part challenge, part invitation. The second dru halted but a few steps away. He glanced up briefly, uncertainly, hazel eyes growing wider as his gaze took in the spread of Rory's branches, the majestic bulk of his trunk; then his eyes focused once again on Kieran.

The reverence with which the lad regarded the holly was as obvious as it was understandable. In his human form Kieran was stunning. Long limbs. Lean, sinewy muscles. His bare skin was winter-pale. His hair, dark as a crow's back for the most part, was laced with starlight threads. And his eyes, as Rory well remembered, were the deep, pure green of a pine forest reflected in a moonlit lake.

The unknown dru stared longingly at Kieran. His hazel eyes held a stormy mix of doubt and desire. "Your Majesty?" He addressed Kieran hesitantly, clearly eager for more of his attention yet reluctant to overstep his bounds.

Kieran made no answer. Arching his back, he stretched his arms high above his head and rubbed his body provocatively along the length of Rory's trunk. His action pulled a needy groan from the young oak's throat, but that was nothing compared to the effect he had on Rory. Desire thrummed along every fiber of his being. The slide of Kieran's skin against his bark was a sensuous caress, but one he could barely feel—enough to tease, but never enough to satiate. All at once, Rory was aware of his own desire, of the need to feel his lover skin to skin. A tremor ran through him—until even his branches shivered.

A small smile played upon Kieran's lips as he too glanced up at Rory's crown, where the tremble was most obvious. Mischief sparkled in the depths of Kieran's eyes. He grabbed his would-be suitor by the wrists. "Tell me your name again, lad?" Kieran urged as he tugged the lad flush against him.

"Fionn, sire," the lad replied, sounding breathless.

"Fionn," Kieran repeated, lips and tongue caressing the

single syllable, drawing the sound out slowly as though it were a new flavor whose taste had intrigued him. "Ah, yes. Now I remember." Then he used those same lips and tongue to sample Fionn's mouth.

Rory could feel the pleasant weight of both men as it rested upon his trunk. Another shudder swept him, root to crown as a thought occurred to him. How much more pleasurable would it feel to have Kieran pinned between them like this if Rory were in his human form? If he could but remember how to wrest himself free, perhaps he might join them and find out.

A whimper broke from the young oak's lips as Kieran continued to explore his mouth. Fionn wrapped his arms around Kieran and held him in a tentative embrace. Heat roared through Rory as desire turned into need—a need to lock his arms around his lover; for lips and tongue—aye and teeth as well—to mark the strong curve of his neck; for a cock to thrust between those pale globes of flesh that, even now, were being ground against his hardness.

Kieran broke off the kiss with an impatient sound. Then, with a swiftness that clearly startled the near-to-swooning oak lad, Kieran slid out of Fionn's embrace and quickly reversed their positions. Now it was Fionn who found himself pressed face-first against Rory's trunk; Fionn, whose fingers clutched at his bark.

Rory chuckled silently. The lad's expression suggested he was surprised by this turn of events. He shouldn't be. As Rory had discovered aeons ago, when dealing with the Holly King, one should always expect the unexpected.

Kieran dropped to his knees behind Fionn. This time, a tremor tore through both oaks when Kieran took Fionn's ass in both hands and spread his cheeks. With his mind still partially embedded in the Greenworld, Rory was surprised to realize he could share what the other drus were feeling. And with his memory supplying the missing details, he could easily imagine what it would be like to be Fionn right now, to be on the receiving end of Kieran's touch.

The hot wind of Kieran's breath set them both to shivering. Rory felt as though that sensuous breeze was painting over his own skin as well. When Kieran's tongue swiped over Fionn's sensitive flesh, drawing a pained cry of, "More. More. Oh, give me more," Rory would swear it was his own phantom pucker that had clenched in response.

The holly took his time. Again and again he speared Fionn's hole, first using just his tongue, and then gradually adding a couple of fingers. Until Fionn was left pleading for release, and Rory, blasted by the rush of sensation, found himself incapable of thought. Every flick of Kieran's tongue, every twist of his fingers, each move was calculated to drive Fionn mad with need. And each one found its mark. Of that, Rory had no doubt. Fionn's reactions alone would have proved it, but Rory could also feel the echo of each sensation resonate within. It was, perhaps, not quite as maddening at this remove, but Kieran was nothing if not thorough, and little by little Rory could feel himself being brought to his knees, if only metaphorically, by Kieran's ministrations.

Finally, content with his preparations, Kieran rose to his feet in one graceful, unhurried motion. Once again he cast his gaze upward, briefly—as though to assess Rory's response. Kieran's cheeks were flushed with arousal, and though his eyes were partially veiled, Rory was certain he saw smug satisfaction gleaming in the depths of those green orbs. Had Rory still harbored any doubts as to whether Kieran was aware of his reaction, if he'd wondered at all whether Kieran's intention was to tease *him* to distraction, right along with Fionn, that look would have removed them.

Ah, but you'll pay for this, my friend, Rory promised silently. Yes, Kieran would pay—would pay in kind, if Rory had aught to say about it—for visiting such delicious torment on him, but not just yet. At the moment, Rory was content to remain where he was. More than content, in fact. Why had they never considered doing this before? He felt as though he were in both men's bodies, sharing the experience from both their perspectives, and from his own as well, as though it were he caught in the middle, caught between them. When Kieran pressed against Fionn's back, positioning himself just so, Rory felt the heat of him, as Fionn must, all along his own spine. When Kieran reached around Fionn's hip to wrap his fist around the lad's cock, Rory felt that too. He shuddered with Fionn's reaction, all the while sharing Kieran's understanding, knowing he was acting to protect the tender flesh, to shield it from being abraded by Rory's bark—even though it made his own hand vulnerable.

When Fionn moaned low in his throat as he thrust his hips back and ground against Kieran, Rory felt his own groin throb from the pressure. And when Kieran finally began to thrust himself inside Fionn's body, Rory was both the penetrator and he who was penetrated.

Kieran barely made the breach; then he paused, head cocked to the side as though listening for something. Fionn gulped for breath. "My lord! Oh, sire—Kieran—please!"

Kieran tightened his grip on the boy's cock. "Hush," he commanded in soothing tones as he stroked slowly, teasingly, up and down the length of it. He leaned closer, licked at Fionn's ear, stroked him a few times more. He canted his hips and gave another shallow thrust, sinking only another inch into Fionn's body. Then he stopped again. "Don't move until I give you leave to."

Fionn bowed his head in submission. "As my sire commands," he said, his words almost lost beneath the sob that sounded as though it had been wrested from his chest. His fingers dug into Rory's bark as though he would tear it loose.

Rory groaned silently. What mischief was Kieran up to now? He marveled at Fionn's control. How did he stand it? The burn, the stretch, the spreading heat—they all demanded movement. Were Rory in Fionn's position, he'd have long since lost patience with this game. He'd have thrown Kieran to the ground by now, climbed atop him, and slammed himself down on Kieran's waiting cock. Even in his incorporeal state, it was all Rory could do to keep from pushing back with his hips to force Kieran deeper. Kieran kept up his torturous pace, slowly opening Fionn up to his invasion. Pausing occasionally to stroke the lad's cock or pull at his sac, to whisper praise or soothing words—yet all the while refusing Fionn's repeated pleas that he be allowed to move, or be given more, or that Kieran would move faster. By the time Kieran had finally seated himself balls-deep within Fionn's arse, the young oak was shaking and sobbing, begging to be taken; and Rory was inwardly writhing, desperately seeking the magic that would set him free. Only then, only when he'd finally succeeded in reducing both his lovers to incoherence, did Kieran begin to move.

If Rory had had lips, at that moment, he would have echoed the groan of relief that broke from Fionn. The pleasure was exquisite, almost a match for the bliss he'd long suspected the Forestmind would give him, were he to allow himself to be absorbed fully into it.

Taking pleasure. Giving pleasure. Both at once. As Kieran pounded into Fionn with swift, smooth strokes, Rory sank ever deeper into the experience. In his mind, he was caught in between the two men, thrusting and writhing, grinding and clawing, calling out endlessly for more.

Rory felt it mere seconds before it happened. Fionn's muscles seized, and Rory's gut tightened in response. Fionn threw back his head and cried out Kieran's name as hot stripes of steaming seed splashed against Rory's bark. Rory shuddered, wishing for his own release. It didn't come, not surprisingly, but all the same, his mouth watered with the all but overwhelming desire to taste Fionn's essence.

And then Kieran was coming as well, and Rory was distracted once again from his own needs.

With one hand still clutched around Fionn's softening cock, the other braced against Rory's trunk, Kieran bound them all together, uniting them. His eyes were closed. His head was bowed. A helpless whimper left his throat as he came—so desperate and needy it caused an answering ache to blossom deep within Rory's heart.

Something inside him tore free at the sound of Kieran's distress, and Rory reached out once again for the magic through which he might free himself. He could think of nothing but leaving his tree and wrapping his arms around Kieran's form, of holding him close and gentling him with kisses. Yet even as Rory worked his spell, he could feel Kieran pulling away from him.

Kieran slipped carefully from Fionn's body and then turned and pressed his own back against Rory's trunk. Breathing hard, he stared up into the branches, his eyes distant, his expression unexpectedly bleak.

Fionn raised his head to look at him. Perhaps he saw some of the same vulnerability that Rory had spied, for he straightened at once and reached for Kieran. "My liege?"

"That's enough now." Kieran brushed Fionn's arms aside and then pushed him away. Not exactly unkindly, but with a firmness that did not invite Fionn to try again. "I thank you for your time, and for sharing yourself with me, but I need you to leave. Now."

"S-s-sire?"

"Go," Kieran repeated, an uncomfortable expression on his face. He gave the boy another small push. "There's a good lad. Off with you now."

A deep flush rose in Fionn's cheeks. His eyes widened in hurt dismay. "But… if it pleases, Your Majesty, I would…I would stay awhile longer. If I might?"

Kieran's expression hardened. He said not a word, just continued to gaze pointedly at Fionn until the lad bowed his head.

"As my sire commands," he murmured as he turned away. "Rule well, Your Majesty," he added, his words but a whisper. Then he headed off down the hill.

"My, you're a cruel one," Rory chided as he stepped from his tree, materializing at Kieran's back, inserting himself magically into a space that had not even existed a moment earlier. He bent to kiss Kieran's ear. "I do not believe I've ever seen this side of you before."

"Which side is that?" Kieran asked. He wrapped his hands around Rory's forearms, where they crossed over his chest. A sad smile glimmered faintly on his lips. "And why, pray tell, do you call *me* cruel?"

"Why, the lad's besotted with you, Kieran. Did you fail to see it?"

Kieran's shoulders sagged. "I saw."

"And yet you brush him off so coldly? There is a hardness about you I had not remarked before. No wonder you rule the year's dark half. "

Kieran shot Rory a sidelong gaze. "Exactly. It is in my nature. I cannot imagine why you would expect me to behave otherwise. But why are we talking about me? When it's *you* who has kept *me* waiting, who has wasted practically the whole day—all the time we could have had together. Now, when I finally hit upon a plan to gain your attention, you dare complain about the methods I employ?"

"'Twas not your methods to which I was objecting—far from it, in fact. 'Twas the way in which you chased that lad off so quickly afterward. He might have stayed."

"Ah." Kieran's jaw tightened. The hands that clutched Rory's arms clenched a little tighter. "A thousand pardons, my liege," he replied in peevish tones. "I had not realized you had an interest there. If you wish to go after him, you are welcome to do so. I, of course, will not be joining you at this time, since I have other matters to which I must attend. But, please, do not inconvenience yourself on my account. I am sure you'll be able to catch up with him if you hurry. He cannot have gone too far."

"Quiet," Rory ordered. Indeed, he was sure the younger oak had not gone any distance at all. He'd be very surprised if the lad wasn't loitering somewhere in the bushes, spying upon them, even now, listening to every word they spoke— and likely praying he'd hear something kinder about himself than he was likely to given the strangely hostile note in Kieran's voice.

Rory didn't know what to make of that. It couldn't be

jealousy, could it? That emotion had never had any place in their relationship with each other. With only a handful of days per year in which they might be together, neither of them could afford to be exclusive. Yet, all the same, this felt…different, odd, unsettling somehow, almost poignant. He shook his head and said, "I'll not be chasing after anyone at present."

"I'd offer to play the role of procurer for you," Kieran continued. "If you feel it's beneath you to do so yourself. But alas, I must plead off. My time here grows short, after all."

"Aye, that it does. But you're not going anywhere, just yet." Still holding Kieran close, Rory flexed his hips and ground his erection against him. "And definitely not till you've finished what you've started."

Kieran pushed out of Rory's embrace. "Why look to me for such service, O king? The woods are surely filled to overbursting with drus who'd be both willing and honored to assist their monarch with his needs."

"No doubt," Rory agreed. "But, as it happens, I do not want any of them. I want you."

"Indeed?" Kieran's gaze turned haughty, but his eyes gleamed with wicked challenge. "So then, 'tis I who is to be distinguished by your interest—is that the way of it? And for what—all of a quarter of an hour? You overwhelm me."

Rory chuckled. "We've done the deed in less time than that, have we not? And if you choose to consider it an honor, so be it. In truth, I care not. 'Tis not your honor I'm interested in at the moment, Kieran, 'tis your arse. So get it over here. Now."

"Oh, very well." Kieran raised his eyes heavenward and sighed. "Since you've asked so nicely." But then his smile broke free. He hoisted himself into Rory's arms, locking arms and legs around him, and kissed him hard. "But we need be quick about it—alas, that is no joke. No more wasting time in useless chatter. There's been far too much of that as it is."

Rory sighed. Kieran's weight felt so right in his arms. All

he could think about was getting inside of him. Turning, Rory pressed Kieran against his tree, determined to have him, right then and there, but then he paused. "No, wait. This won't do at all." His hoary bark was far too rough. Unfortunately, the ground was little better, being mostly barren rock. "You'll tear up your back like this."

"I'll do no such thing," Kieran scoffed. Then, without so much as a flicker of an eyelid, he magicked a long black velvet cloak. It clasped around his neck and fell from his shoulders and down his back, cushioning him against the bark. "Better?"

"Barely."

Kieran rolled his eyes. An instant later, he'd added a soft white shirt and a thick leather jerkin as well. "And now?"

Rory bit back a groan. "It will do." He supposed he shouldn't argue—the clothes were his idea after all—but even though the sight of Kieran, half-clothed like this, with his lower half still bare, was decidedly erotic, Rory would have much preferred to have him naked in his arms. "Come winter, I shall have you on your back on a downy featherbed. I shall keep you there, or on your knees, throughout the entire solstice, and I'll not allow you any clothes at all."

Kieran's indrawn breath was shaky. His face flooded with color, and he lowered his eyes in a show of submission that Rory suspected was mostly faked. "As my sire commands."

Faked or not, Kieran's words drew a growl from Rory's throat. He leaned in and nipped at Kieran's jaw, then took his mouth in a brief kiss—all they had time for. The taste of him was at once familiar and strange. Rory knew it must be Fionn he was tasting there. Again, an errant pang of jealousy surfaced. Winter, he promised himself as he broke the kiss. *Winter, featherbed, no clothes, Kieran.*

"Suck my fingers," Rory ordered in a voice made gruff with need. "Make them wet for me."

Kieran happily obliged, eyes gleaming as he drew Rory's fingers deep, as he tickled the spaces between them with his tongue and nipped at the edges.

"Enough." Rory pulled his fingers back. "Now, make yourself hard. We've not much time, as you keep reminding me, and I'll not last long anyway, once I get inside you, but I want you coming with me."

Kieran groaned. He closed his eyes, leaned his head back against the trunk, and did as he'd been told. Rory stretched and teased Kieran's opening, until the holly was panting in his arms and he himself could barely breathe for all the tension within him—a tension that was only made worse when Kieran's legs, still locked around Rory's waist, began to tremble. Unable to wait any longer, Rory pulled his fingers from Kieran's body. He thrust into him, seating himself fully.

"Ah, Rory." Kieran's whisper was as much a sigh of contentment as it was a plea for more. Rory gave it to him, pounding into him hard and fast, grateful after all for the sturdy leather.

All too soon it was over. Kieran broke first, and the hot jets of seed as they splashed against Rory's belly, the strangling grip of Kieran's muscles all around him, were more than Rory could resist. He thrust himself deep and poured himself into Kieran's body.

Kieran lowered his head to Rory's shoulder. Rory locked his arms around the smaller man and held him close. Peace and contentment filled his heart. But only for a moment.

"Let me down," Kieran said, his voice tight.

"It can't be time already?" Rory protested, even though he knew that it likely was.

"And yet, it is," Kieran replied, his eyes averted. Rory let him down. The instant Kieran's feet touched earth, his clothes disappeared.

"This is my fault," Rory blurted, wishing suddenly, urgently, for that which they could never have, a lifetime spent in each other's arms. "And I'm sorry for it. I wish now that I'd been more timely."

Kieran brushed his apologies aside. "Think nothing more of it." A smile graced his lips. "But I tell you now, I won't wait as long next year to awaken you. And I'll not just bring that young man you seem so enamored of with me either. Next time, I'll rustle up a couple of wood nymphs as well. I'll throw an orgy right here on the ground at your feet. And if you choose not to join us in our debauchery, it will be entirely your loss."

"Indeed, I shall look forward to it," Rory promised with a laugh. "But thank the gods we need not wait a full year. I shall see you in December." *Winter, featherbeds, Kieran.*

Kieran nodded. "Aye, that you will. And I shall use whatever magic I possess to bend time and give us what we need."

Rory smiled. "All I need is you."

They held each other's eyes as the wind rose up around them, a sudden, crisp breeze, spicy and dry, with a hint of ice and a taste like apples. It wrapped itself around Kieran's form, and when it died down again, he was gone from sight.

Rory sighed. "Rule well, O king." Then he turned his head, listening. There was no movement in the brush around him, not a leaf stirred, not a twig seemed out of place, but he knew this grove and he was not deceived. "I know you're in there. Come out, now, and show yourself."

A frozen silence met his words, followed a moment later by an exhale of breath, a slight rustle in the undergrowth. Fionn got to his feet. His expression was wary as he approached. Eyes downcast, he fell to his knees at Rory's feet.

Rory studied him for a moment in silence. He was young but strong, sturdy, dependable. His countenance, when first Rory spied it, had been radiant. Now there was an air of sadness about him, a tinge of grief. Rory could easily guess what that was about. "How long have you been in love with our Kieran, then?"

Fionn glanced upward in surprise. "All my life," he blurted, then bowed his head again as a flush stained his cheeks. "That is to say, we both hail from the same grove, Your Majesty. My tree stands not that far from his, you see, and…and…"

"Ah, yes." Rory nodded. "I am very familiar with Kieran's grove." His heart contracted in pain as he thought of his own grove, as it once had been, all the trees he had known... "A very fine grove it is, but not the largest. I imagine you couldn't very well help but notice him under those circumstances, could you?"

"No, Your Majesty." Fionn shook his head, his face still downcast, his expression one of abject misery as though he were expecting Rory to issue a warning, or an order perhaps, to demand that Fionn keep his distance from Kieran in the future. It unsettled Rory to realize how much he wanted to do just that. Instead, he stroked the boy's hair, the sun-kissed curls so springy to the touch, as he fought against unexpected jolts of jealousy and lust.

He could doubtless have the boy, if he wanted him— Kieran had been right about that—and he did want him. Though Fionn had little of Kieran's delicate prettiness about him, being far more rugged, he was still a beautiful young man. Memories of his recent tryst with Kieran still filled Rory's head. And here the lad was, the same who had given himself so willingly to Kieran, kneeling sweetly in submission before him. It was all Rory could do to restrain himself.

He was on the verge of reminding Fionn that Kieran would not return until winter, of suggesting ways in which they both might entertain themselves in his absence. But then he remembered the odd, hurt tone in Kieran's voice. Somehow, he didn't think the holly would like it if Rory dallied with this boy. He did not understand why that should be the case, but in his heart he knew it to be true. And that was enough to stop him.

He took hold of Fionn's curls and tugged, forcing the boy to meet his gaze. "Do not look so glum, young oak. You both have many years ahead of you. It is clear you've caught his interest now. That fact alone should give you cheer. After all, one needs start somewhere. Is that not so?"

"S-sire?" Fionn stared up at him earnestly, heat and a

faint trace of hope in his eyes. His tongue flicked nervously at his lips, and Rory felt his noble intentions begin to slip.

Without thinking, Rory drew his thumb across Fionn's lower lip, tracing the path the boy's tongue had taken. "And after all," he murmured, surprised by the husky timbre of his voice, "Kieran and I cannot be together always; why should we not enjoy the company of others in between times, as we have always done?"

A shudder rocked Fionn's body. Heat flared in his eyes, and his mouth opened slightly in unspoken invitation. Rory hurriedly recollected himself. He released his hold on the lad's hair. "Well then, seeing as Kieran's gone now, I guess there is no sense in your hanging around here any longer, is there? If you are smart, you'll go and find something else with which to entertain yourself for the time being."

Some of the tension left Fionn's frame. His cheeks blazed red as he bowed his head once again. Rory told himself the disappointment he read in Fionn's eyes was nothing more than imagination.

"Yes, Your Majesty," Fionn murmured dutifully as he rose to his feet. "Of course."

As the boy turned to leave, Rory called out to him again. "And don't go looking for him the minute the solstice releases him either. I promise, I'll be keeping him busy for as long as I can, and I don't want him distracted by anyone else. Let him search you out, instead. If you find it galling to be forced to wait, I bid you recall that life is long, and some things are worth the wait. You'd be well served if you cultivate some patience."

Rory couldn't help but smile as he watched Fionn depart. He had little doubt Kieran would be looking the lad up again, and why should he not? Fionn was everything an oak should be—steadfast, loyal, strong of heart. It pleased Rory to know there were still such in the world, even if they were not from his own stock. It was enough that the species itself would continue. "He'll do," he murmured as he too, turned away from what was left of his grove and headed off to find his own entertainment. He had six months of freedom to enjoy, and Kieran again, at the end of it.

FIONN'S KNEES WERE shaking as he left the Oak King behind. He'd been certain he was about to be reprimanded, if not punished. Allowing himself to be fucked right against the Oak King's tree was disrespectful, to say the least. They'd been asking for trouble. But that was what Kieran had wanted, so Fionn had made up his mind to accept the consequences. However Rory chose to discipline him, Fionn would not repent his actions.

Still, kneeling there on the rocky ground, his face just inches from the Oak King's groin, Fionn knew exactly what kind of penance he'd *hoped* he might receive. He could smell the older oak's musk, mixed with hints of Kieran. It was heady, intoxicating, irresistible. Fionn had been lusting after Kieran ever since he was old enough to understand what lust was. He'd always known his desire for the Holly King was a hopeless dream…until all at once it wasn't.

Rory, though… As High King of the Drus *and* Lord of the Forest, he was even further beyond Fionn's reach. The moment should have been intimidating. Instead, Fionn's mouth had been watering. All he could think about was wrapping his lips around the great king's cock.

It was an impressive size, even when flaccid, and Fionn had been dizzy with the thought of it—and that was even before Rory took hold of his hair! Fionn's heart began racing in anticipation of what was surely coming next.

Any moment now…

And the only question on Fionn's mind had been whether or not he'd be allowed to grasp hold of those heavily furred thighs to anchor himself as his throat was plowed.

What a turn his day had taken! What a marvelous change of fate. When he'd awoken this morning it was with the unhappy knowledge that, after today, he'd not be able to catch even a glimpse of Kieran for another six months. Now, he was on the verge of having been taken by both kings in one day. He grew giddy just thinking of it. To have had one of their cocks in his arse, the other in his mouth. Why, the only thing better would have been to have had both of them at once; to be surrounded by that much power, that much strength.

For a moment, he'd been lost in his fantasy. He'd imagined himself on all fours; rocks biting into his hands and knees; his cock bobbing stiffly in front of him, so hard it hurt; long strings of precum extending down to the ground. Rory's hand would be twisted in Fionn's hair as he guided his cock toward his mouth. Kieran's fingers would dig sharply into Fionn's hips as he dragged him roughly back and forth. Back, until he was fully seated in Fionn's arse. Forward, so that Rory's cock could fill his throat.

"Very good, young prince," Rory would praise, his gravelly-toned voice demanding surrender. *"Open for us. If you would someday take your place among us, you must first prove yourself worthy."*

And Fionn would have groaned and whimpered and let himself be used.

It had been something of a letdown to realize Rory wasn't interested in anything of the sort. It had been humiliating as well. Fionn was certain the Oak King had known exactly what he'd been thinking. That was even worse than having been so summarily dismissed by Kieran. For, as Rory had been kind enough to remind him, at least he had succeeded in capturing the Holly King's attention. Now, all he had to do was figure out some way to keep it.

In the end, Fionn had not approached Kieran in December—nor in January, February, March, or even April. He was aware of him, of course. Fionn had *always* been aware of Kieran. But he held himself aloof, not willing to approach the Holly King too soon. He told himself he was simply following Rory's instructions, but in truth, it was more than that. He was holding out. In some tiny corner of Fionn's heart burned the irrational hope that maybe he wouldn't need to go in search of Kieran, that perhaps the

Holly King would find him first.

By April, Fionn was forced to admit that was not going to happen. And by the first of May, he'd resigned himself to the all too likely possibility that Kieran had forgotten all about him. The next step, therefore, would have to be his.

* * * *

Kieran could not help but flinch when he recognized the soft voice that hailed him.

"I bid you a good Bealtaine, my liege."

Bealtaine—of course. A holy day dedicated to sex and fertility. Kieran could barely disguise his dismay. He really should have seen this coming. He turned toward the speaker, already knowing what he'd find. Fionn. With a smile on his lips and an eager, hopeful expression in his eyes. Kieran had seen that look before, and he knew all too well what it meant. Time and again in the last few months, whenever their paths chanced to cross, he'd noticed the lad watching him hungrily. He'd known Fionn was waiting for Kieran to speak, to acknowledge him, to say *something*. But Kieran already felt bad enough for having led the young oak on last summer. The last thing he wanted to do now was encourage him further.

When March and then April had passed without incident, Kieran had grown complacent. Was it unreasonable to hope that Fionn had finally moved on to other interests? Apparently it was. Kieran should have recalled the extraordinary guilelessness of oaks, their constant, steadfast hearts—so very different from his own dark, twisted soul. Rory had been quite right about that.

"And a good day to you, as well," he replied, striving to keep his voice as noncommittal as possible and refusing to use the lad's name. Let him think he'd forgotten it; it was better that way. Guilt stabbed at his heart when disappointment washed the smile from Fionn's face. He found himself unbending enough to ask, "I trust you've been keeping well?"

A simple enough question, Kieran had thought, yet Fionn beamed radiantly in response. "Y-yes, Your Majesty! Quite well, and you?"

"Splendid." Kieran nodded and, offering Fionn a tight smile, began to turn away. Fionn stopped him again.

"Excuse me, Your Majesty, but I was wondering…"

"Yes?"

"I was wondering if I…if I might be of any further assistance to you, my liege?"

Kieran's cock sat up and took notice. It was all he could do to keep from groaning aloud. Damn him for a fool. He really should have seen this coming. Because, yes, Rory was proved right again; the lad *was* besotted, and Kieran had known it.

Fionn's feelings for him were obvious—had been from the start. And that alone should have made him totally off-limits. Kieran had never suffered from any lack of lovers. He'd shared his body with many others over the years. He knew Rory had done the same. But it had always been understood that his body was all he shared. Kieran's heart belonged to Rory; and that was all there was to say about that. Whether the reverse was true, was not important. As a relatively short-lived holly, Kieran could never expect to outlast an oak. And that suited him just fine. Not for Kieran the role of grieving lover, crippled by loss, unable to function. Even if the unthinkable were to occur and he did find himself alone, he could never imagine loving anyone else.

Still, it was with regret that Kieran shook his head. "I thank you, but no." Fionn needed to move on. He should have done so by now. "Flattering though it is—"

"Perhaps another time?"

Kieran glared. Did the boy even realize he'd just interrupted his king? How dare he?

"I'm sorry, Your Majesty," Fionn continued in a rush. "It's just that, when last I spoke to his majesty, he did say that I should—"

"His majesty?" This time it was Kieran who interrupted, practically blinded by sudden, unreasoning jealousy. "You spoke to Rory? About *me*? When?"

"Why, last summer, my liege."

Kieran's jaw clenched. Oh did he? It was odd that Rory had made no mention of that fact last December. He'd certainly enjoyed teasing Kieran about Fionn and his infatuation, warning Kieran that, if he wasn't careful, Fionn would likely pine after him forever. Aye, and he'd had plenty to say, as well, about Kieran's allegedly coldhearted treatment of the lad. At the time, Kieran had assumed Rory had been speaking in jest, that he meant less than half of what he'd said. That his sole intent had been to watch Kieran squirm. Now he wasn't so sure. Was it possible Rory had meant every word? Might he not have come to prefer Fionn—someone young and pure and lighthearted, someone with whom he might spend more than just a handful of days every year—over someone as inconvenient as Keiran, someone he'd already described as cold, hard, and dark?

Did that question even need an answer?

Fionn was still speaking, but Kieran waved him to silence. "It's of no matter to me what either of you said to one another, or when you said it, or at what length the two of you spoke. I've no interest in any of it. All you need know is this: I have no need of your assistance, nor shall I in the future. So please do not importune me again."

Then, paying no attention to the look of hurt surprise on Fionn's face, Kieran brushed past the lad and continued on his way. Perhaps he was doing the lad a disservice, but if Kieran was right in his suspicions, if he really had lost Rory's regard, it was best for Fionn if he kept his distance. Kieran had never been a gracious loser. He did not envision that ever changing.

And if he was not right? Well, harsh as it may seem, he was still convinced that a swift blow now, sharp and clean, would be better for Fionn in the long run.

Chapter Three

December 1839
At the time of the winter solstice

Ice crunched beneath Kieran's feet as he climbed the hill to stand beside the ruined oak. The sky above was dark and hard, and a light dusting of snow lay on the ground, but everything else looked just as it had the last time he'd stood there six months prior. Blackened bark and charred wood showed where lightning had split the trunk apart. The once proud crown still lay as it had then, bending low to touch the ground. Shriveled, half-formed leaves still clung to the branches, though they were brittle now and brown, no longer the same tender green they'd been when the spring storm had swept down upon the hill with deadly intent and gale force winds, when lightning had danced upon the earth, when life had ended.

Kieran laid his hand again upon the shattered wood. That too was much as he remembered it, only more dry now, more cold, more dead.

Why, then, was he still so surprised? Why did the tears still spring to his eyes? Hadn't he known it to be so when he stood here last summer, when he'd begged and pleaded and received no response? Had he not spent the past six months frantically searching the Greenworld, seeking any sign that the soul he cherished was not completely gone?

Six months and nary a whisper to hold on to. Still his heart refused to accept what his senses told him was true. Still his feet had brought him here again today. Still his heavy heart beat to the same stubborn, hopeful tattoo: it was not too late. It *could not be* too late. He had magic. He had hope. He had to try…something.

How could the world survive without its Oak King? How could *he* survive? How was it possible that there was no way to fix this, even now?

He was a creature of the In-Between, that place without place and time out of time where all the hidden edges of the world connect. If Rory still lingered anywhere between life and death, surely Kieran could find him?

Raising the magic within him, Kieran laid his hand over the exposed heartwood. He closed his eyes and cried aloud. "O Lord of the Forest, you who rules the waxing year, you who brings life to the world, I summon thee! O Mighty Oak, you who are first of all trees, reveal yourself! Come here to me now! The season has changed. Your reign awaits. The world needs you." He swallowed hard and then added quietly, "I need you. Please."

A gentle breeze touched Kieran's face, warm and sweetly scented. Hope blossomed. His heart beat fast. He hardly dared breathe as his ears picked up the sound of...yes, of footsteps climbing the hill. Could it be? Oh, please, let it be!

"My liege?"

The voice that spoke behind him was a familiar one, but it was not the one he ached to hear. Kieran's hopes shattered anew. He spun around. Scarcely able to contain his fury, he scowled at the young oak who stood before him. "You! Have I not told you to stay away from me? How *dare* you approach me here?" This was hallowed ground, sacred to the memory of he who'd once stood here. Kieran could not bear for any other feet but his to tread upon this earth.

Fionn gazed back at him sadly. "I'm sorry, my liege." He cleared his throat and added, "I would not have intruded upon you in your grief, not for anything in the world, but sire...'twas *you* who...'twas you who summoned *me*."

Kieran seethed at the implication. "I did no such thing."

Fionn averted his eyes. If possible, he looked even more miserable than before. "I fear you did, sire."

"I did not, I tell you. Never. I..." Kieran felt himself pale as Fionn's meaning became clear. *The king is dead; long live the king.* No. Impossible. "Are you saying that you...that *you* would pretend to take *his* place?" The very thought was insupportable. Had Kieran not just expended all the magic currently at his command, he would craft such a spell it would blister Fionn's skin.

"It seems most unlikely, I know. Why, I can still scarce believe it myself. 'Twas only this Samhain that our blessed Lord and Lady did appear to me—"

"Oh, did they? Prove it then. How did they look? What did they say to you?"

Fionn stilled, gazing off into the distance, his face dreamy with remembrance. "Beautiful they are, fair beyond all imagining. Their eyes are wise and benevolent, unfathomably deep, filled with the knowledge of everything—past, present, and that which is yet to come. Their voices... In truth, I do not know, even now, if they were speaking aloud, or only in my head. For the sound of them was everywhere at once, softer than a baby's breath, more powerful than the ocean when it rages. As to their garments—I cannot begin to tell you what it was they wore, for those were almost too bright to gaze upon. They glimmered as though they'd been woven of moonbeams, and the jewels in their crowns outshone the stars."

"Stop." Kieran sighed in defeat. "I've heard enough." He felt betrayed. It was inconceivable that the Lord and Lady could be mistaken about *anything* and yet... In place of Rory, they would give the world this...this untried youth to rule them? How could they?

"I would that it were otherwise," Fionn murmured quietly. "Believe me, I would change things if I could."

"You are *nothing* compared to him."

Fionn sighed. "I know it well." After a moment he asked, softly, "But...will you not aid me in this? Will you not help me become what I must? Will you not tell me what to do?"

The immensity of what was being asked of him overwhelmed Kieran. He drew in a sharp breath as memories crowded in. To be forced to relive that time in his life when he'd been at his most vulnerable? To revisit his own desperate sense of being unequal to the task assigned to him?

To recall Rory as he'd been then—so kind, so compassionate, such a bulwark of strength; to remember all the qualities that made Kieran fall in love with him, and to do so now, when his heart was already sick with grief? "No." He could not. He couldn't bear it. He closed his eyes against the pain.

"Please, my liege," Fionn begged softly.

Kieran shook his head. "You need do nothing. The wind will find you. The Forestmind will claim you. You need only...allow it." It was hardly that simple, of course, but Kieran's heart tore apart a little more as he remembered his own first time, how endlessly patient Rory had been with him, how gently he'd helped to prepare him.

There was much that Kieran could say to Fionn right now; much that he, perhaps, *should* be saying, but the words wouldn't come. He was not the dru Rory had been. Nor was Fionn, for that matter. Nor was *anyone.*

"The wind," Fionn repeated in hollow tones. "I remember."

"Do you?" Kieran couldn't help but laugh at the trepidation in Fionn's tone. But it was a sad, cold sound, lacking in both humor and comfort. Even he felt the chill of it. "Oh, well then, I imagine you know something of what to expect." Had Fionn witnessed the wind take him...when would that have been? Two years ago? Three? No matter. Viewing it from afar was nothing compared to experiencing it yourself—especially not the first time. Kieran knew he ought to warn Fionn about that. That he ought to be supporting him somehow, not making light of his fear.

But hot tears had gathered behind his eyes blinding him to anyone else's pain. "You'll be all right," he said, at last, forcing the words out. "Just let it take you. It will anyway."

Fionn nodded stiffly. "Very well then. If that's all you have to say, then I... I apologize for having troubled you. I will take my leave now."

Swallowing hard, Kieran averted his gaze. He was aware he was failing Fionn, but he couldn't help it. His soul felt as burned and blackened as the dead stump before him.

Remorse was just one more emotion he was unable to summon. Then another thought occurred. "One last thing. Never come here again. A great king once stood upon this hill. I would consecrate this ground to his memory. I will not have him be forgotten."

Fionn's eyes narrowed. He opened his mouth as if to speak, but before he could get so much as a single word out, the wind arrived. His face turned ashen. But Kieran barely noticed the mute appeal in the young oak's gaze as it locked with his. For in that same instant, a scent like summer, soft and sweet, had wafted over the hill and Kieran's breath had caught as cruel hope twisted his heart once more. *Please. Let it not be over. Let this all have been but a terrible mistake...*

The wind rustled briefly in the leaves of the fallen tree, a lingering caress, like a lover's last touch. *Please!* Then the wind moved on. The leaves fell still. And that gentle finality cut Kieran's legs out from under him. A sob tore from his throat as he collapsed on the ground, weeping, at the foot of Rory's tree.

Chapter Four

Fifty-five years later
June 1894
At the time of the summer solstice

The woods were shadowed, tranquil and green as Aine Murphy made her way into the forest. This early in the day the sun had yet to burn off the morning mist, but although the day promised to be fine, an unidentifiable melancholy seemed to hang in the soft, still air. It was just a trace, but enough of one that Aine took note of it and thought it strange. Why should the forest feel so gloomy today? What grief dared mar so perfect a morning?

When she reached her destination, a secluded grove where a stately young oak and wizened holly stood a short distance from one another, she paused and glanced around, feeling the hair rise on the back of her neck. The sense of sorrow, of loss—of despair, almost—was even stronger here. She did not consider herself a fanciful woman, but there was an unusual sentience in the woods today. If she didn't know better, she'd swear she was being watched.

She shook her head, waiting for the odd notion to dissolve. It was naught but foolishness. She was well aware that there was no one to see her. Indeed, that was another of the reasons why she'd chosen this particular place for her ceremonies; it was as far from her neighbors' prying eyes as she could get. She brushed her concerns aside and set about getting ready for the morning's ritual, taking comfort in the familiar routine—the same one she'd followed for several years now, ever since her husband's death had freed her to worship as she saw fit.

She began by setting up her altar, reverently laying out the tools she would be using. Then she walked the circle, calling on the directions and raising power as she went, carefully placing eight stones around the perimeter to denote the quarter and cross-quarter days. When she'd returned to the start point, she stopped and removed her cloak. Cool air caressed her bare skin, raising goose bumps on her arms and legs and pebbling her nipples. A hush seemed to fall over the forest. The feeling of being watched grew stronger.

Her heart was beating uncomfortably fast as she entered the circle and knelt upon the soft green moss. She'd come here today to sing songs of praise; to greet the newly crowned Holly King and pay homage to the fallen Oak—a ceremony that had always brought her joy in the past—but the atmosphere this morning had unsettled her. No longer in the mood to tarry, she rushed through her opening prayers and started right in on a hymn in honor of the Oak King. She was midway through the second stanza when her ordinary day caved in upon her. A naked stranger materialized from out of the fog, nearly scaring the life out of her in the process. Aine gasped in surprise. "Gods save me."

The stranger said nothing. He stared back at her, looking almost as surprised as she. For one shocked instant Aine was convinced she'd somehow conjured the very Spirit of the Forest. Then reason reasserted itself. This was no insubstantial sprite—his heavy muscles and gleaming flesh attested to that. However godlike he appeared, he was likely no more than a no-account rover, a drifter who'd stumbled drunk onto her property the night before and judged this sheltered grove to be a perfect place to catch a night's sleep.

"Who-who are you?" she demanded shakily, still staring at him. "Whence did you come?"

His chestnut hair was shaggy and overlong, streaked gold as though by the sun and in desperate need of a trim. It hung in his face, very nearly obscuring his beautiful hazel eyes. Even partially veiled, those eyes were remarkable, a warm amber color overall, like honey and cinnamon swirled together, but with bright flecks of summer green shimmering in their liquid depths. His strong brown body was broad and tall. Perhaps not quite a match for the oak tree that spread its branches above their heads, but still he was an impressive sight to behold. He quite captivated her attention. Although, given that they were both skyclad at the time, their mutual surprise was not so astonishing. She, at least, had a cloak with which to cover her nakedness.

"Answer me," she demanded as she scrabbled for her cloak and hastily wrapped it around her. She was pleased that her voice no longer shook, though her heart was still pounding at far too swift a pace. She should be running away, but she feared her legs wouldn't carry her.

"There's no need to fear me, lass," the stranger said, smiling in a way she suspected was meant to be reassuring. "I mean you no harm."

Aine's mouth tightened. "Sure, and wouldn't you like me to think so?"

The stranger blinked and appeared confused. "I would, indeed. Why else would I have said it?"

Aine choked back a laugh. Her hands were shaking as she began to gather her tools together, spilling everything repeatedly, her motions too jerky and uncoordinated for anything else. "Why indeed."

"Here, now." The stranger took a step closer. "Let me help you with that."

"No!" Aine raised her hand in a futile effort to stop him. "Stay back. Do not come any closer."

"As you wish."

His easy acquiescence emboldened her. She stopped what she was doing to level a glare at him. "What I *wish* is that you'd see fit to answer my questions. Who are you and what are you doing here?"

FIONN DIDN'T ANSWER right away. If truth be told, he was having trouble finding his voice. It wasn't just that Aine's beauty stole his breath; he was also dazed and disoriented, momentarily depleted of power. Who knew it took so much effort to work magic? Well, Kieran, probably.

But, then again, Fionn suspected there were many things the Holly King knew but had not bothered to share with him.

Bitterness rose inside him at the thought, at the memory of Kieran's cold disregard. Although most of the hurt Fionn once had felt had long since turned to anger, the old resentment smoldered still. If there was one thing he would *not* be wasting time on—neither now nor ever again, if he were lucky—it was Kieran.

Now that he had finally broken free, Fionn intended to live as a human, at least until the winter solstice. Perhaps he wouldn't go back at all. Maybe, if he were truly lucky, he would discover that the winds could not find him on this side of the veil. Or maybe, in his absence, his Lord and Lady would choose someone else to take his place, someone better suited to the task than he.

"Answer me," Aine demanded again. Despite the hint of steel in her voice, her eyes were huge and her breath was shallow and far too fast.

Is she still frightened then? The realization that, yes, apparently she was, struck at Fionn's heart. It didn't help him find his words any more quickly. Aine had always seemed supremely confident, like a goddess in the flesh. He hadn't thought his appearance would cause her more than a moment's startlement. He hadn't thought of...well, entirely too much, obviously, damn him for a fool.

He'd acted on impulse, thinking only of his own needs, making a mess of things—as usual.

But that merely served to strengthen his resolve, that was yet one more reason why he'd been right to take this step and leave the throne behind. If he could not live up to even his own expectations of how the Oak King should behave, why continue? Why not try and carve out a life for himself somewhere else—here, for example—where no one had any expectations of him at all?

"My name is Fionn. I heard you singing."

"And what of it?" Aine's chin rose. A hint of challenge hardened her gaze. "Why shouldn't I sing? This is all private property. You would not have been in a position to hear me if you were not where you've no right to be in the first place!"

"Indeed, I can think of no reason why you should not sing," Fionn replied. "In fact, I wish you would continue. Your voice is as beautiful as your song."

Her voice *was* beautiful, beautiful, honest, clear, and she'd been singing to *him*, though she did not yet know it, sweet words of love, honor, and respect, when all he'd had elsewise for year upon year was censure. Her song had been balm to his wounded soul, a lure he could not resist. "It's what brought me here."

"And? You think me a witch now, I suppose. Is that it?"

"A witch? Not at all. More like a goddess."

Aine snorted derisively. "Ah, listen to the man. A goddess, am I? Such nonsense!"

Fionn cocked his head to the side as he studied Aine's expression. Though she shook her head, as though his words had been displeasing to her, Fionn could tell by the color in her cheeks that she'd liked them. "'Tisn't nonsense at all. Certainly you sing like a goddess. I don't think I've heard anything more lovely than the sound of your voice."

"Well, I thank you for the kind words, however undeserved they be." She finished packing her things back together—moving a little less frantically now, he was pleased to see—then got to her feet. "But now, whoever you are—"

"I told you. My name is Fionn."

"So you did. Well, *Fionn*, I—"

"And you are named Aine."

She stared suspiciously at him. "Who told you that?"

Fionn felt his own eyes widen. "No one told me. It's true, is it not?"

"Yes, but…h-how do you know? Who've you talked to about me?"

Fionn shrugged. "No one. It's just…" He could hardly tell her the truth. He could hardly say that he'd been observing her for years, slowly falling in love, until the thought of never actually speaking to her face-to-face, never touching her, never even really getting to know her, had become a source of pain, an all-but-impossible burden to bear. He could not always be throwing his heart away unheeded. "This is not the first time I've seen you."

"That is no answer at all!"

Embarrassed, Fionn glanced away. "You interest me. Please, can we not leave it at that? I would very much like the chance to learn more about you."

"Oh, would you? Well, seeing as we're on the subject, what *I* would very much like is for *you* to get off my property. Go back to wherever it is you have come from. And, for the love of heaven, before you do so, put on some clothes! My neighbors think little enough of me as it is. I can only imagine what they would say if they were to see you leave here looking like that!"

Fionn frowned uncertainly. "Is there something amiss with my appearance then?" Her words sounded so harsh, yet the gleam in her eyes, the flush on her cheeks, had led him to believe she liked what she saw.

"Other than your nakedness, you mean? No, that would be the sum total of the problem."

Fionn felt a shaft of disappointment pierce his heart. So it was true then; his looks did not appeal to her. What was it about him that she found objectionable? Did she think him too large, too plain-faced and brute-like? Maybe she'd prefer someone more elegantly formed—more like Kieran, perhaps—with his lithe build and delicate bones. Fionn could hardly fault her if that was the case. Unbidden, images of Kieran sprang to mind, but Fionn beat them back. The Holly King was nothing to him now.

He cleared his throat. "I apologize. It had not occurred to me that you would find the sight of me so displeasing." If he had, would he still have taken the risk to come here? He couldn't honestly say. "But...may I at least hope you will not turn me away based on looks alone?"

"Displeasing?" Aine covered her mouth as she was seized suddenly with a fit of coughing. "Oh, dear heavens."

Fionn gazed at her in alarm. "Are you ill?"

"Ill!" She gasped and shook her head, still sputtering uncontrollably, and was unable to speak for almost a minute. "No, you impossible man, I am not ill."

"Well, then?"

"Oh, never mind. Just get dressed! Do, please. I beg you."

"Alas, I fear I cannot." Could one even wield magic in the mortal realm? Fionn didn't actually know. That was yet another detail he had failed to consider.

"And why can you not?"

"Because, much as I would like to oblige you, I have no clothes with me." If he'd thought about it, he might have attempted to magick himself the proper attire before breaching the veil. But would the clothes have made it through with him? He had no idea.

"What now?" Aine frowned. "Of course you do. You must. Where are they? Go and get them! At once!"

Fionn shrugged. "I cannot."

"Ah, sure and you must be mad," Aine murmured. "Or I must be, for listening to you." She narrowed her eyes and studied him a moment longer. Finally she seemed to come to a decision. "Very well. Since you clearly cannot stay as you are, you may accompany me back to my house. I will give you some clothes and then see you on your way. Come along."

As she headed out of the grove, Fionn fell in step beside her. "Would you send me away so soon then? Even knowing I have nowhere else to go? Will you not at least sing to me once more?"

Aine shot him a sidelong glance. Before she could answer, an eerie wailing sound rose up all around them, startling Aine who jumped and clutched at his arm. "Gods preserve me. What was that?"

Fionn forced a smile. "'Tis naught, sweet lady. The wind, perhaps."

"The wind!" Aine scoffed. "Of course it's not! What

manner of wind could it be that sounds like that, and yet disturbs not so much as a single leaf?"

Fionn seethed quietly. How very like Kieran to interfere. But how dare he do so? It was not like he had an interest there himself. For years, the two kings had had naught to say to one another. Whenever Fionn chanced to see him, Kieran had been cold and remote so that a little more of Fionn's heart had shriveled up each time.

He shook his head, once again pushing all thought of the Holly King to the back of his mind. Then he took hold of Aine's arm. "Come now, my dear. Whatever it is, it hardly matters. 'Tis sure I am that it will cease to bother us once we're well away from this place." Then, using his grasp on her elbow, Fionn propelled her along the path—out of the woods and away from Kieran's prying eyes.

* * * *

Bound in his tree, unable to move, Kieran stared after Fionn in furious, fearful disbelief. What was the fool doing? What was he *thinking*?

Did he somehow imagine that the veil that kept the realms apart had sprung into being by accident? Not true! There was a reason it had been erected, a reason the dru had chosen to hide themselves away from humankind.

For someone to do as Fionn had just done, to throw off the defensive magic with which they and their kind had kept themselves safe for centuries, and in clear view of a mortal woman, no less... It was unconscionable, unimaginable, dangerous.

To be sure, the woman in question might well be worth the danger, but all the same...

Does he wish to die? Is that what he wants? Does he wish to see us all dead?

Aine. It wasn't as though Kieran had never noticed her before himself. She was, after all, one of those humans, rare in these modern times, who still clung to the old ways, a fact that could not help but endear her to even Kieran's hard heart. But in the dead of winter, the time when he'd been most aware of her, she'd always come to the woods bundled against the cold. That had made it easier for him to underestimate her appeal and ignore his own attraction to her.

This morning, revealed in all her glory, gazing up at Fionn in wonder and rapt surprise, she'd been as impossible to ignore as the sunrise.

She had looked undeniably lovely kneeling naked on the cushioning moss, and Kieran had been all but overcome with longing. He had intimate knowledge of how it felt to lie with another on that earthy bed. He knew the kinds of green and vibrant scents that would rise from the bruised moss as two bodies struggled together, rolling about on the ground, laughing and joyous, striving together for release. He knew the breathless pleasure that came with surrender, when one of the pair ceased in his struggles and gave in to the other's will. He knew what it was to follow the order implied in a pair of hard, sweat-slicked thighs when they wrapped around his hips, urging him to bury his cock ever deeper into the hot, moist fissure of another's body.

But, up until now, all his experiences had been with those of his own kind. Until this morning, when Fionn's actions had all but forced him to consider it, Kieran had never even allowed himself to flirt with the idea of taking a *human* lover, much less a woman. Why even the males of the species had always seemed far too shockingly delicate.

Ah, but Aine...

Her long red hair had been unbound, the thick wavy locks hanging almost to her waist, partially concealing the tight pink tips of her full, round breasts. Her narrow waist had fairly cried out for a man's arm to encircle it. Her rounded thighs would feel like heaven as they cradled his hips.

Her milky skin was heavily freckled, giving her the look of a dappled fawn, an impression that was only reinforced by her wide-eyed gaze. Even as he watched, her skin pebbled up, either with cold or fear; Kieran had no way to tell which. It hardly mattered. He wished it was in his power to go to her either way, to offer shelter, protection, reassurance, warmth—whatever she might want or need or think to ask him for. Anything she wanted, he would gladly provide, in exchange for the nurturing sustenance of her kiss...

Ah, but such thoughts were madness! Kieran could hardly account for them. They must be due to the fact that it was now summer, that season when the Greenworld was at its most fecund. All of creation was alive, yearning for completion, aching to join with one another in that most ancient of dances. It had ever been that way.

With his soul immersed in the Greenworld and all the power of it flowing through him, it was little wonder Kieran's thoughts should have trended in so earthy a direction. And he could hardly fault Fionn for succumbing to the same attraction he himself was feeling. But if Kieran *could* have moved at that moment, he would not have been rushing to join Fionn, but to stop him. If he could have spoken, he would have begged the younger man to reconsider.

However blameless or sympathetic she might appear to be, Aine was human and not to be trusted. Worse than that, as the current caretaker of this bit of land, she held the life of these woods—Fionn's woods, Kieran's woods—in her hand. With a single word she could have their small grove cut down and destroyed. Kieran had seen it happen before. There were already too few woods left on this little isle, and every empty field spoke to him of man's greed and lack of foresight.

Surely Fionn could be made to see reason—or at least stopped from making any more mistakes? But Kieran was unable to act. He could not intervene, could not offer counsel. He could only watch.

It had been years since he'd felt this helpless.

And if Fionn should happen to find himself in some trouble from which he could not extricate himself in the next six months—what then? Well, he would not be the first oak whose loss Kieran would have had to endure. He'd lost one king already.

No. That will not happen. I will not allow another to be taken from me.

Fine words, Kieran reflected bitterly, but they were meaningless without the wherewithal to back them up. As the Forestmind drew deeper on his consciousness, pulling him inexorably into the quiet decay that was the dark half of the year, Kieran had time for only one final realization, one last thought, and it was of Fionn.

For the briefest of moments this morning, the Oak King had captured Kieran's attention, forcing him to look—really look—at the younger man in a way he had not done in a very long time. Perhaps 'twas true what he'd often heard said, that sometimes people failed to realize what they had until it was already gone.

Chapter Five

What was I thinking? Aine scolded herself, a short while later, as she bustled about in her kitchen fixing breakfast. *I'd no right to be bringing that rascal home with me. I am like to be murdered in my bed, I am. And 'twould serve me right an I were.* But the mere thought of bed—with Fionn just steps away, in the small spare room off the parlor, changing into a set of Patrick's old clothes—was enough to bring the blood flooding to Aine's face. She shook her head at her own foolishness. Aye, she was daft, all right. There was no other explanation.

When they'd gotten back to the house, she'd made Fionn wait downstairs while she went up to her bedroom to dress. She'd donned her clothes as quickly as she could, keeping her eye on the door the whole time, ears straining for any sound of him climbing the stairs. When she was finished, she'd gone to the chest where she still kept some of Patrick's clothes. As she'd riffled through them searching for something appropriate, she did her best to ignore the faint pang she felt whenever she recalled her late husband.

Patrick had been a good man—she could not say aught against him. He'd treated her well while alive and left her comfortably situated afterward. But once her grief at his passing had lessened—and it had lessened far sooner than she'd felt comfortable admitting even to herself—Aine had found she had neither the wish nor the want to remarry. No man was so good, or so she judged, that he was worth giving up her independence for.

She was not afraid of hard work, and if there were tasks she could not handle on her own, she could always hire someone to help her. If she needed a man to warm her bed at night, or perchance by day…well, that might be a bit more problematic. But were she to set her mind to it, she was sure she could find a way to deal with that as well. Doubtless her good neighbors would be scandalized had they been privy to her thoughts, but no more so than they would be were they to find out what she'd been up to in the grove this morning.

She wasn't sure what Patrick would think of her actions either. She knew he'd disapproved of what he'd termed her heathenish customs, but surely he wouldn't begrudge her giving his clothes away to someone who so clearly needed them.

Not that she understood how Fionn had come by that need. Mayhap he'd been the victim of foul play, though one would think he'd have mentioned the fact if he'd been an *innocent* victim. Or perhaps he'd thought the miscreants who'd made off with his garments—and his money perhaps, and who knew what else besides, were friends of his, playing a prank, and he was embarrassed to admit he'd been played for a fool.

Whatever had brought him here, however, 'twas madness to continue the association an instant longer than was necessary. Any sensible woman would have shown him the door once he was decently dressed, thanking the saints that she'd suffered no harm, relieved to be finally rid of him.

But had Aine done so? No, she had not.

It had occurred to her as she was handing him his clothes that they'd likely both missed their breakfasts this morning. It would hardly be charitable to send the poor man on his way without at least offering him the chance to sit and have a bite to eat. The invitation to do so slipped past her lips before she'd had a chance to reconsider. And the smile it brought to Fionn's face could have lit up the room.

"Indeed, I will. And gladly."

The sight of such naked joy fair took her breath away, so that even after he'd disappeared into the other room to dress, she still stood there staring at nothing, quite mesmerized.

It was more than just his smile that was affecting her, it was everything at once—from the timbre of his voice, to the warmth in his gaze, to the desire that shone, clear and ready, in his eyes. Everything about him promised pleasure. Her pleasure. More pleasure than she'd ever known or even imagined possible.

As she went about the task of making breakfast for the two of them, she could hardly keep her thoughts contained. Like a colony of rabbits set loose in a field, they raced away in every direction. Yet, ever and again, they insisted upon returning to that first glimpse she'd had of Fionn rising naked from the grass to tower above her, each muscle so clearly delineated. The fresh dew-scent of him so intoxicating it made her mouth water. Each time she remembered it, she could not keep her breath from hitching, nor herself from wishing that the two of them were both naked still, stretched out together on the welcoming moss...

* * * *

Fionn picked at the remnants of his breakfast. He was pleased Aine had deigned to share her meal with him, even though she'd done so with seeming reluctance, but he was more than a little bemused by the experience. Human food was something of a revelation; he'd never known anything like it. His connection to his tree was what sustained him. As long as his tree was alive, absorbing light through its leaves and water through its roots, he had no need for other forms of nourishment. Up until now, he'd no cause to sample it. But this morning, pleasure alone gave him reason to indulge—pleasure and the need to make the most of his time with Aine.

Since she'd started coming into the woods, nearly a decade ago, she'd become the sole bright spot in his year, the one thing he had to look forward to, as he'd once looked forward to catching even a glimpse of Kieran. He would do anything to win her—and certainly sharing a meal with her was no hardship! He only wished he felt equally enamored of yet another human custom she'd insisted upon, namely the wearing of clothes. Fionn would gladly do whatever Aine required of him. He would happily give her whatever she requested, and gratefully accept anything she was willing to offer him. But why did that have to include clothes?

So far, he had to admit, the practice did not recommend itself to him. Wool itched, he had discovered; even linen, a fiber with which he should have been more in harmony, felt stifling. The fact that said clothing had originally belonged to Aine's husband, now deceased, only added to Fionn's discomfort.

Thinking now about the loneliness he'd always sensed in Aine—a longing for something that could never be attained, a sadness he wanted desperately to assuage—he knew he should have guessed there was someone whose loss she mourned. For had he not known those very same emotions? Not that the man he'd loved was dead, of course, but he might as well be. Fionn's hopes for the two of them certainly were.

"I still don't understand how it is you knew my name," Aine said suddenly, her gaze wary, her voice uncertain. "I keep coming back to that, and it worries me no end. You said you'd seen me before. When exactly was that?"

Fionn took his time answering. "I don't recall exactly. But there have been several times, over the years."

"When? Where?"

"Whenever I have had occasion to be in yon woods. On the solstice, in particular."

"In...in *my* woods?" A fiery blush heated Aine's cheeks. "Are you saying you've spied upon me there—in the one place where I felt safe to shed my clothes without fear of embarrassment or molestation? How dare you, sir?"

"Your woods? Is that what you call them?"

"Yes, mine. Whose else would they be?"

Fionn held his tongue. The woods in question were his woods too. Indeed, from his perspective, they were a good deal more his than hers. But that was not a discussion he wished to have. "Fine, then. Call them what you will. But why should you not shed your clothes—there or elsewhere? What reason have you to feel embarrassed by your nakedness?"

Aine scowled. "Of course *you* would think that. You're quite content to go around in naught at all!"

"Exactly. For that matter, nor would I term what I did 'spying'."

"Yet another point on which we must disagree." Aine shook her head as though disgusted. "So tell me, other than the solstices, when else have you been around to spy on me?"

Fionn tamped down his own temper. "Once again: I do not spy. I pray you will cease saying so. My being here was...unavoidable. 'Twas never my intention to upset you. And, in answer to your question, yes, it has mostly been at the summer solstice that I've seen you. I am, perforce, elsewhere for much of the year."

"Oh, indeed? Well, perhaps you might take yourself elsewhere now?"

"Aine." Fionn gazed at her reproachfully. "Surely you do not mean that?" He rose from his seat and hurried round the table to kneel by her chair. His heart clenched in sorrow when she shrank away from him. "Beautiful lady, do not fear me. Surely you know by now there is no cause to! If you truly desire me to leave you, I will go at once. Never think otherwise. But, please. Will you not reconsider? I beg you; do not send me away so soon."

"Stop!" Aine gazed at him unhappily. "What are you asking me for? Why should I let you stay? How can I? You're naught but a daft stranger who can give no accounting of himself. And I am a foolish woman, mad to have let you in at all!"

"No, no." Having finally succeeded in capturing her hands, Fionn brought them to his lips. "Not mad," he crooned as he laid soft kisses on the knuckles of first one hand, then the other. "Never think it. Search your heart. You know it is no such thing."

"Do I?"

"You know you do." Fionn raised his gaze to lock with hers. He smiled, allowing the truth of his words to sink in, allowing the power of his presence to make itself known to her. He was the Oak King. For years she'd made her prayers to him. Surely some part of her already knew and loved him, just as he knew and loved her. His mind pressed gently against hers, urging her to give in to those feelings. "Over the years, I have felt your bright spirit calling to me. Your heart. Your song. Your beauty. 'Tis you who have brought me here."

Aine stared speechless at him for a moment longer. Then she sighed and looked away. "You say these things, these mad, impossible, ridiculous things, and I can think of no reason why I should believe you."

"And yet you do."

"Aye, fool that I am," she muttered, shaking her head. "I do not for a moment understand it, but...perhaps I've been more lonely than I've realized. I want so much to believe you. You cannot conceive how much I long for...for everything you seem to represent."

"And you cannot conceive how much *I* have longed for *this*." Releasing one of her hands, he tenderly caressed her face. "How much I have longed for *you*."

Tears sprang to Aine's eyes. "I am a fool," she repeatedly roundly. "A fool! And yet..."

"Yes, dearest?"

Aine sighed, shoulders sagging as she surrendered. "And yet, just being near you fills me with such joy."

A weight seemed to lift from Fionn's heart. He smiled. "Dearest Aine—"

"No," Aine murmured. She bit her lip and blinked rapidly, trying to look away again, trying to break the connection between them. "Do not. Please do not."

Fionn's hand on her face kept her gaze right where he wanted it, trained on his. "Why so sad, my love? You say I bring you joy, yet all I see are tears."

"Because..." Aine's voice trailed off. She swallowed hard and tried again. "Such feelings cannot last. I have known love and I have known loss, and it seems to me that the two are oftentimes two sides of the same tarnished coin. You can never have one without t'other, it seems, and—"

"Stop." Fionn silenced her. "I too have known loss. But those are matters for another day. For today, you need know only this. I came here for *you*. And, if you will have me, I would remain with you for as long as fate allows."

"I will have you," she said, going into his arms without another word of protest.

WHY SHOULD SHE not have this? Why should she not take him to her bed, right then and there? Those were the questions that hammered at Aine's senses, and she could not for the life of her produce a reasonable answer. Why should she not give in to the heat and the need rioting within her? They were both unattached, unencumbered, answerable to no one but themselves. So why should they not comport themselves however they pleased? And how better to honor the spirit of the solstice than for the two of them to strip naked once more and reenact the Great Rite itself? No one had ever made her feel this way, alive and wanton, aching with need, yearning for life and heat and passion. It was Fionn whom she ached for, longed for, needed. It was for him that her sex ripened and swelled, all for him. She hardly knew him, and yet somehow...somehow she did.

And, somehow, she knew it was he for whom she'd been waiting.

Perhaps the fault lay in the fact that she'd neglected to complete her ceremony. Perhaps that was the cause of this insanity. All that wildfire energy she'd raised this morning was still blazing away inside her, addling her senses. She could think of nothing else that could account for the way she was feeling, more alive than ever before in her life.

Whatever the cause, she was determined to grasp it with both hands and hold on to it for as long as she could.

Fionn wrapped his arms around her and then stood, bringing her up with him. He carried her over to one of the chairs that bracketed her hearth. He sank into it and settled her on his lap. Smiling, she framed his face with her hands and kissed him, loving the way his hands tightened convulsively at her waist, loving the taste of his mouth, and the way her name sounded on his lips. "Aine."

Good as it was, however, it wasn't enough, so she squirmed around until she straddled him. He slid his hands up almost immediately to capture her breasts. Meanwhile, she was already busy unfastening his pants. She was a little shocked by her own efficiency at undressing him; she'd never been so bold before. By the time Fionn had undone her bodice and freed her breasts, she had his pants wide open and was already reaching for his cock. His shaft was thick and hard and mapped with veins. She stroked slowly up and down his length, enjoying the sense of power it gave her to touch him so freely, to claim him as her own...but it was still not enough.

"Oh, Aine." Fionn groaned as she slipped from his grasp and then sank to her knees between his legs. Finally, she thought, as she ran her open mouth up the length of his cock. She used her tongue on all his most sensitive parts—the plump head, the dripping slit, the thin membrane that stretched beneath his crown—teasing him before she opened her lips once more and swallowed him down.

FIONN SLOUCHED LOWER in the chair, spreading his legs wider to give Aine better access to his straining cock, making it easier for her to slide her hand in underneath and cup his sac. He watched as her head bobbed up and down, and briefly considered climaxing in her mouth. The wet heat of her tongue gliding over his glans, the fluttering tightness of her throat muscles as she took him deep were surely the most exquisite sensations he'd ever known. But he needed more. He needed to touch and taste her too. Every part. Needed to commit it all to memory, every sight, every sound, every flavor, every curve. For who could say how many such pleasures the two of them might share?

He tightened his hold on her hair and tugged. Aine paused. Raising her head, she gazed up at him questioningly, eyes dark with heat, her lips so swollen and red.

He groaned impatiently. "Come here to me now. I need to bury myself inside you."

An eager flush stained Aine's cheeks as she clambered back into his lap once again. Fionn slid a hand beneath her skirts, seeking the split in her undergarments that would allow him to finger her slick and swollen flesh. "How wet you are," he murmured, his voice thick with need, sighing with pleasure as he buried one finger deep inside her snug passage. He pulled out, then dragged his finger back and forth through her folds, circled the sensitive little pearl, using her juices to paint over her heated flesh.

"Now," Aine ordered impatiently. "Please!" Fingers trembling, she guided his shaft to her opening.

Ever obedient to her wishes, Fionn slid both hands beneath her to cup her soft flesh and hold her open. A low groan rumbled in his chest as she sank down on top of him, slowly engulfing him in her heat. She clutched at his shoulders and used her grip there to steady herself as she began to ride him.

"That's it, love," he murmured approvingly, as he matched her rhythm, gripping her hips and stroking into her. She blinked wordlessly at him. He loved the dazed look in her heavy-lidded eyes, loved the tremor that rocked her, loved knowing it was his words that caused it. He'd say anything to put that look on her face, to make her shake like that, to watch her teeth worry her lower lip as they were doing now. "Let me serve you. Use me for your pleasure."

Aine gasped. Her hands shook. Her nails dug into his shoulders. Fionn leaned in and took one berry-red nipple in his mouth. Her sex closed like a fist around him as she surged against him.

The rippling of her muscles all around his cock was too much for Fionn. Abandoning finesse, he tightened his grip and rocked hard into her. His climax flashed through him like lightning, swift and blinding...and over far too soon.

It took a moment longer for the storm to pass, but

eventually their hearts stopped galloping, their breathing returned to normal. They pulled away, each of them taking a moment to readjust their clothing. Then Fionn pulled her back against him. He clasped his arms loosely around her waist, already missing the closeness, the warmth of her snug in his arms.

Never enough, never enough, never enough time...

Chapter Six

The September sun felt good against Fionn's skin as he worked the soil in Aine's garden, using his magic to coax the plants to grow strong and fast and continue to bear fruit even as the seasons turned. Such had always been his purview. It came naturally, and he derived much satisfaction from it. True, the harvesting of said crops still seemed foreign to him, but it brought such joy to Aine that he strove to understand it for her sake.

As he paused in his work to drink some water from the earthenware pitcher Aine had provided him, he turned his face to the sky and closed his eyes to better enjoy the moment with all his senses. He luxuriated in the pleasant heat radiating from the solar orb, in the gentle play of the wind in his hair, the contented clucking of Aine's chickens as they scratched in the dirt looking for bugs, the quenching coolness of the water, the scent of the good earth all around him. And—most of all—in the newfound peace that filled his heart, that sense of having finally found his place in the world.

To be sure, he was not unaware of the irony—that maintaining this blissful state was largely dependent on his continuing to deny his true nature—but at the moment, that seemed a small price to pay. He was thrilled with his new life. He wanted to capture each precious moment, trap it in amber, and keep it forever. But how was such a feat to be accomplished?

Aine was blossoming for him. Every day she seemed a little more carefree, more playful and relaxed. It was a joy to watch. When he'd first arrived, her heart had been so tightly curled upon itself, like a bud too fearful of the weather to unfurl. She'd been beset with worries, doubting his motives in wanting to stay with her, troubled by thoughts of what her neighbors would think if he did.

Fionn had found her concerns largely incomprehensible. Why would he not wish to stay with her? And what did it matter what others might think? In the end, he'd been forced to expend a fair bit of magic there too, in his efforts to ease her fears. While he'd been gratified by her reaction—and by the realization he could still access his magic on this side of the veil—it did add to his concern for the future.

What had he really accomplished by journeying here? He'd hoped he'd be allowed to relinquish his duties, to be set free from his responsibilities. Responsibilities that anyone could see he was not cut out for. Why, Kieran had even said so!

But thinking about his kingly counterpart did nothing to improve Fionn's mood. It wasn't true that he had come here to avoid Kieran's censure. It wasn't the Holly King he was running from. But, at times, it felt like it was.

Fionn had grown up in Kieran's shadow. His childhood hero worship had turned into a boyish crush as he got older and then into a not so boyish crush when he reached adulthood. When Kieran had chosen him on that summer's day so long ago, it had been the fulfillment of a dream—of every dream Fionn had ever had, at that point. It hadn't occurred to him he was merely being used, but even if he'd known, he would have gone ahead just the same, pride be damned. Even after their tryst had ended so abruptly, he'd continued to lust after the man, as anyone might. But once Fionn was named king—and Kieran's equal—he'd been forced to give up those dreams.

How could he be the equal of the man he wanted so badly to submit to? How could he bow his head in obeisance, offer himself for Kieran's use, and still consider himself worthy to wear the Oak King's crown? How could he ever again acknowledge his feelings for Kieran, never mind give in to them, without hopelessly disrupting the balance of power between the two kings or without further undermining his already uncertain authority?

Equals? Ah, that was a joke, it was, and he the butt of it. The two of them were no more equal than they were both mere daisies, nodding at one another in the grass. Kieran was every inch a king, strong and crafty, possessed of all the power and wisdom that came with age, as well as all the grace and charm that befitted his station. Yes, he could be cruel at times, arrogant and careless with his attentions, but that perhaps was only to be expected. In comparison, Fionn felt callow and unready, too hasty, too clumsy, too green—even now, over half a century later.

It helped not at all that he could not even begin to fathom why they should be deemed equal to start with. By rights, should he not be the stronger? He was oak, after all, chief of all trees. By any logic he could think of he should certainly outrank the holly, which was neither tree nor bush, but something altogether different—a creature of the misbegotten 'Tween.

It seemed all wrong that Fionn should be forced to surrender his crown each June, while all the energy of the summer was flowing through him, while he was at the very height of his strength. Was he a willow that he should bend, that he should abase himself or grovel at Kieran's feet? Why should he not proclaim his dominance, stand tall and proud and refuse to yield? He should be demanding Kieran's respect, not bowing down before him. Not craving his affection or longing for his touch. No wonder the Holly King despised him so.

It wasn't as though Fionn didn't know how a proper king should act either. On that summer day, when Kieran had so unceremoniously dismissed him, Fionn hadn't slunk away immediately as Kieran no doubt had expected. Anyone with even a scrap of pride would have done so, but not Fionn. Instead, he'd hung around for a time, skulking in the brush, nursing his humiliation and—even more humiliating to remember now—spying upon Kieran in hopes he might, perchance, change his mind.

I don't spy, Fionn had promised Aine. Oh, but once he had—and only to his sorrow. He had witnessed for himself how the old king dealt with Kieran, how quickly and completely he'd put him in his place. And that was at the summer's turn. That was the oak in defeat—still strong and magnificent, still commanding respect. Nothing at all like Fionn.

A simple life, an unexceptional life—a life spent here, as a human, as a farmer, with Aine by his side—that's all Fionn wanted now. Was that really too much to hope for? In his heart of hearts he knew it was. He was still the Oak King, after all. And if the winds could find him at the solstice, they would surely take him. Once he was gone, what was to stop Aine's heart from freezing over once again? What was to stop her being lost to him forever?

A commotion among the chickens captured his attention. The rooster was attempting to corral one of the hens who'd ventured too far from the flock for his liking. Fionn could not help but laugh as he watched their antics. The squawking hen kept evading the rooster's best efforts to herd her in the direction he wished her to go. He felt a distinct sense of kinship with the beleaguered rooster. When it came right down to it, was he not approaching Aine in the exact same way, frantically dodging this way and that, trying to assuage her fears, to prove his love, to keep her from turning away from him? If it wasn't even working for the chickens, whatever made him think it would work for the two of them? If he really hoped to win her heart, he'd be far better off approaching her as a human might.

The thought stopped him in his tracks. Why could he not approach things as a human? True, he'd only lived among them for a very short time, but he thought he understood something about their customs. They put their trust in words as much as deeds and, above all else, in promises exchanged. When it came to matters of the heart, he knew exactly how they proved themselves to one another.

* * * *

Aine was preparing their midday meal when Fionn arrived back at the house. "Well, you are in early," she said as he strode in through the kitchen door.

Instead of answering, he grabbed her around the waist, lifted her up, and swung her around in a circle, before finally saying excitedly, "I've had an idea!"

"Have you?" She smiled back at him. "What is it, then? Tell me."

The past three months had been impossibly grand, like something out of a dream. They'd been the happiest of Aine's life—and all because of Fionn. He'd calmed her fears and soothed her worries. He was a treasure—one she'd do anything to keep. When he'd happened to mention, several weeks into their acquaintanceship, that he had an affinity for the Greenworld and all growing things, she'd been pleased to offer him a job helping out around the farm. She hadn't expected much to come of it, but his ability with plants had proved to be nothing less than amazing. If his newest brainstorm was anything like the last, she couldn't wait to find out.

Fionn put her back on her feet before answering, "We should marry."

Aine swayed on her feet and had to lay a hand on Fionn's arm to steady herself. "What?"

"Marriage," Fionn repeated, continuing to beam at her. "You know what that is, do you not? It's where I pledge my love to you, and you do the same for me, and we both agree that whate'er else befalls us we'll never truly be parted this side of the grave."

Marry Fionn? Aine's initial reaction was one of disappointment. She'd made up her mind several years ago that she would never be married again. Surely she should stand by that decision. She should not go back on her word now, even if her word had been given only to her own self. But, on the other hand, at the time it was decided, she hadn't had Fionn to factor into the equation. And it was certainly one way to solve some of the issues she'd been wrestling with since midsummer, like how to keep Fionn *and* her reputation. How to still her neighbors' tongues. How to keep the man she suspected of being an itinerant wanderer tied to her doorstep.

When she put the question to herself in that way, there was only one possible answer. "Yes." The word sprang from her lips without another thought, and it felt so right she said it again, just for the pleasure it brought her. "Yes. Yes, I'll marry you. Of course I will!"

* * * *

The village priest was far from enthusiastic when Fionn and Aine applied to him.

"What're ye thinking, my child?" he asked after pulling her aside under the guise of hearing her confession. "You know as well as I do how often I have counseled you on the subject of marriage in the past. You have always claimed to be content on your own; now all that has changed. Why? I know it's not for lack of other offers. There've been plenty of good men who've pursued you, men from right here in town."

"Aye, they did. And yet every last one of them was less interested in acquiring a wife as they were the land I come with. Or perhaps it was a good nursemaid they were looking for, someone who could cosset and care for them, who'd cook their meals and mend their clothes."

"'Tis many a woman would consider it a blessing to have someone to care for."

"Perhaps. But I made up my mind after Patrick died that I'd had enough of it. Good men or no, they may all look after themselves, thank you very much."

"And yet, here we are. Tell me, what do you even know about this man?"

"I know enough," Aine insisted, brushing aside the good father's concerns. Being with Fionn fulfilled her in ways she could not even hope to describe. He made her feel alive and passionate, joyful and complete—what more did she need to know?

"My mind's made up, Father. I'll have Fionn for a husband, or no one at all. Are you saying you'll not marry us?"

The old priest sighed and shook his head. "No, alas, I am not. If I cannot change your mind, then I have no choice but to see you two wed. I do not do so happily, mind you, for I fear you are making a mistake. But I can see how things are with the two of you, and I judge that even an unhappy marriage is better than falling into sin. As I very much fear will happen an I refuse you."

"You make a very good point," Aine replied, refraining from pointing out the fact she'd already been "living in sin" with Fionn for nigh on two months. Sometimes the less said the better.

And so they were wed. And for the first several weeks, Aine was blissful beyond belief. But all that changed a few weeks after Samhain, when winter began to creep across the land and not even all Fionn's skill could keep the farm producing. Fionn's mood turned unexpectedly dark then. Alarmed by the change in him, by the haunted, unhappy look in his eyes, Aine begged him to confide his troubles to her until finally he confessed the truth. Or what he'd claimed was the truth—not that anyone with a lick of sense would've believed him.

It was then Aine wished she'd paid more heed to the good father's concerns. For how was she to believe Fionn's latest claim? She was married to the Oak King? Ah, what nonsense was that?

Chapter Seven

December 1894
At the time of the winter solstice

"Will you not at least look at me?" Fionn begged as he stood beside her in the kitchen, looming over her, pleading for her understanding—as though she were the one who was being unreasonable!

"I will not. So stop asking." Aine kept her gaze trained firmly on the pastry board in front of her, on the bread she was kneading, on her hands as they squeezed and turned and molded the dough. Why she was even bothering, at this point, she could not have said. It was not like they were ever going to eat these cursed loaves—nor anything else that evening. Her appetite was quite destroyed. She was certain she'd never be hungry again. "Just go away now, Fionn, and leave me be. I've heard more than enough of your blather."

"*A mhuirnín*, please. This changes nothing between us. Do you not see that?"

"No, I do not. Maybe it makes no difference to you, but I cannot say the same for myself."

"What else was I to do? You kept asking me for answers until finally I had no choice but to confess. I could not in good conscience keep it from you any longer."

"Your conscience, is it?" Aine snorted in disgust. "Where's your conscience been all these months, then, while you've been keeping secrets from me?" She was glad for her anger, for it kept the tears at bay. And she would not cry in front of him, not even though her heart was broken.

"Perhaps I've explained myself badly. It is not what you think."

"Oh, well, sure and that's a comfort, it is! For what I *thought* was that my husband was naught but a coward, one who would stoop to making up stories—and making a mockery of my beliefs in the process. All in order to excuse the fact he wishes to leave me."

"It is not what I wish! Never that. If I had any choice in the matter, I swear I would cleave to your side forever. But I cannot alter what I am. Would you have preferred it if I were to have vanished without a word, leaving you to wonder what had become of me?"

Aine slammed the lump of dough down onto the counter. Ignoring the cloud of flour that rose up into the air and then rained down upon her, she turned and glared at her husband, her hands fisted on her hips. "What I would have preferred, dear husband, is never to have met you at all."

"Aine..."

"What are you *really*, Fionn? Other than a liar—one way or t'other. For if it's the truth you're telling me now, and I don't for an instant believe that it's even possible, sure and you were lying when you wed me claiming to be a single man, unencumbered. And human, I might add. But whichever is the right of it, it matters not at all. I'm an idiot for believing in you either way."

"I never *said* I was human," Fionn insisted. "You might have assumed that was the case, and indeed, I know you did, but even so I never lied to you."

"Oh, for shame. You've done nothing *but* lie. For nigh on six months you've lived with me and nary a word have you spoken about any of this nonsense until today. What would you call that, if not a lie?"

"I'd say that...for all that I was reluctant to tell you everything there was to know about me, what little I *did* tell you was the honest truth."

Aine sighed. "And I'd say you're obviously one as wouldn't know the honest truth if it jumped up and bit him on the arse. Is it my farm you're after then? For, if it is, be warned. I'll see you in hell before I let you get your hands on the meanest part of it. Or is that not it either? Perhaps the truth is we aren't really married at all. That would explain some things. Have you another wife you're anxious to get back to? I assure you, there's no need to be making up stories if that's the case. She's more than welcome to you."

"I'm a dru. Marriage is... Well, it's not a practice that's common among my people. I have no other wife but you, nor have I ever had, nor do I wish for one."

"Oh, a dru—why, of course you are! And a king too, I believe you said. Is that not so, Your Majesty?"

"Aye. King of the Forest, Lord of the Greenworld, High King of *Éire*."

Something about the way he said it shook Aine's confidence. For just an instant she found herself wondering...? But no. Surely that was impossible.

"I'm not here to take your farm from you, *a rún*," Fionn continued, his voice even gentler than before. "Indeed, my darling, there's nothing here I need or want, or have any stake in at all. Save only yourself and the tree I'm bound to."

Those tender tones and honeyed words would surely break her if she let them. Aine hardened her heart. "Bound to your tree? Is that so? Well, there's a bit of good news at last. Thank you for that. And seeing how that's the case, I've half a mind to have the whole grove cut down. I'll call upon the woodsman tomorrow, I think, and make arrangements. We'll see how that suits you."

Fionn's face turned chalky white. "Aine...no. You mustn't even joke of doing such a thing."

"Mustn't I? Well, I can think of no earthly reason why you should feel yourself entitled to even hold an opinion on the subject of what I must or must not do. And as it happens, I'm not so sure it was a joke. The longer I think about it, the better I like the idea. If I recall correctly, there are several good-sized trees within that grove. Their wood should bring in a nice price once it's harvested and having an extra field to plant never hurt anyone."

"It would mean not only my death, but the deaths of every other dru who lives within those woods. Is that really what you want? Is that of so little concern to you?"

Aine tossed her head. "Even if I believed such nonsense, why *should* it concern me? It's surely nothing more than you deserve. I only wish I could be certain it were really so, for then at least I'd know one way I might be rid of ye."

Before she'd finished speaking, a chill breeze sprang up out of nowhere, raising goose bumps all across Aine's flesh.

"I sympathize with your plight, dear lady," a soft voice murmured, causing Aine to shriek in surprise. "Yet, all the same, I would be much obliged if you'd refrain from carrying through with your threats. In fact, I fear I must insist upon it."

The voice wasn't Fionn's. It was a man's voice though, quiet in tone, yet backed with an edge like hardened steel, and it came from right behind her.

"Gods save me!" In her haste to face the mysterious speaker, Aine spun around too quickly. She lost her balance and went crashing backward into Fionn. He caught her by the arms to steady her, and when she did not immediately pull away, he wrapped an arm around her waist, keeping her anchored in place. She could not say she was too sorry about that either. Angry though she was with him, in that moment she found his solid, familiar heat at her back a great comfort.

Breathless, Aine stared up into the face of the dark-haired devil who'd materialized out of thin air, like the very worst sort of black magic. A pair of glimmering eyes stared back at her, mesmerizing in their intensity. Their color was exquisite too, the deepest green there e'er was, overlaid with silver. At any other time, she'd have appreciated the sight far more than she did right then.

"Kieran." Fionn's voice, harsh and cold with anger, cut through the tension-filled silence. "What are you doing here?"

A mocking smile curved the stranger's lips as his glittering gaze rose to meet Fionn's. "Well met, my liege. I would have thought the reason for my being here was obvious?"

Not quite as tall as Fionn, nor nearly as broad, he was still as handsome a man as any Aine had ever encountered. His hair had been brushed back from his face and reached almost to his shoulders. Like the beard that bracketed his mouth, it was dark as coal, just lightly touched with frost. When he turned his sparkling gaze back upon her, Aine's heart stood still.

"I merely wanted to introduce myself to your new bride, of course, and to wish her happy. But perhaps I have come at an inopportune time?"

"You bloody well know you have," Fionn answered. "And far too soon. 'Tis only the eleventh of the month—ten full days before the solstice. What business have you being here now?"

"Who *are* you?" Aine asked at last, finally finding her voice. "How did you get here?"

The man's smile stretched wider. "I will tell you, since you ask, though I do not expect you'll be pleased with my answers, nor yet believe me."

He'd held out his hand to her as he spoke, and Aine was shocked when her own hand found its way into his grasp without any thought of hers to guide it. A shiver of excitement worked its way up Aine's arm as he lifted her hand to his lips and pressed a gentle kiss against her knuckles.

"My name is Kieran Mac Cuilenn." The stranger's eyes twinkled with mischief. "But I am better known to you, perhaps, as the Holly King. I go where I will and tarry wherever I find a welcome."

"Impossible," Aine whispered. "Impossible!"

"How is it that you doubt me?" Kieran gestured at the holly branch she'd hung above the fireplace. "For, after all, it appears I've been expected. Did you truly intend for me to wait upon your doorstep when you've invited me in by proxy?"

Aine shook her head. This couldn't be happening. Either the two men were telling the truth or they were separate-but-equally daft in their delusions. Or else she'd completely lost possession of her senses and slipped into a dream. Each of these options seemed every bit as likely as the other, and she could not for the life of her decide which of the alternatives she hoped for or feared the most.

"And yet again I say it," Fionn growled. "Why are you here?"

A little of the warmth left Kieran's expression at that, and even his voice turned remote. "Behold, my lord, the wheel of the year is spinning. A new season draws nigh. I have come to yield my crown to you, O King of the Forest."

Fionn stiffened in surprise. Aine felt the tremor that ran through him. "What new mischief is this? You know as well as I do that the solstice has yet to arrive. I still have time."

"Not this year," Kieran replied. "Our days are ruled by both sun and moon. Tonight the winter moon rises full and my rule ends."

"The moon? You must be joking. What care I what phase she's in? Such things do not concern me. 'Tis the sun I am bound to follow, and his circuit is not yet complete. Our reigns are set, Kieran; and have been so for ages. You have no more right to reorder the days than I do."

"Come now, all this arguing is beneath us. I promise you I am well within my rights. By virtue of its placement on the calendar, falling as it does between the old year and the new, Yule is a season unto itself, belonging to neither and yet to both. It is a thing apart, as it were. As such it falls under the purview of the In-Between."

"Over which you *also* have rule, if I recall correctly. I see now how this works. How very convenient for you. But I tell you, I will not have it!"

Kieran's jaw clenched. "Much as it pains me to disagree with you, sire, I fear I must do so once again. I do not 'rule the 'Tween.' Indeed, it suffers no one's rule, for it too is a thing unto itself. Still, those of us, myself included, who are ourselves creatures of the In-Between, who belong to its mystery and share its attributes, are granted certain rights.

While within its sphere of influence we may make use of its fluidity, stretching and molding it according to our wishes and thus shaping it to our needs. Tonight I judged it meet that my reign should end anon. And as I wish it, so it is. Whether you will it or no, you are bound to this duty. It is time."

Kieran's voice rang with certainty and weighty finality, and in response, a low moan of protest broke from Fionn's lips. "No!"

The sound was very like a wintery gale whistling through the bare and brittle branches, so cold and desolate that Aine's heart clenched. Startled, she turned and stared up at her husband. "Fionn?" The agonized look on his face as he met her gaze tore at her emotions. "What is it? What's happening?"

There was a ghostly paleness to his face now, as though the moon itself was shining through it. A sad smile wreathed his lips. "I am leaving, *a grádh*, my dearest love. Though it grieves me terribly, I must bid you farewell. I am sorry that I did not tell you about any of this sooner. I thought I'd have more time to explain it to you. I'd hoped—"

"Stop." Feeling overwhelmed, Aine turned her face away. She squeezed her eyes shut to hold back her tears. "Please just…just stop." She couldn't stand to listen to any more of his excuses, any more of his lies…

And if, as was beginning to seem the case, they weren't lies? How would that change things? Would it make matters better or worse?

Fionn groaned again, eerie and forlorn. "Alas, my love, I cannot tarry, not even to argue with you." His voice was hesitant and sad as he added, "Will you not at least grant me hope that you might think kindly of me when I'm gone, and that when next we meet, you might not turn me away?"

Aine opened her eyes. She hardly dared hope he meant it. She'd assumed this good-bye meant forever. Then again, she'd also assumed he was a lying bastard who'd never loved her at all. Could she really be wrong on *all* those counts? At the moment, she didn't know what to think. It seemed odd to be hoping her husband was not what he'd seemed—to hope that he wasn't even human. And yet, she was startled to realize that was precisely what she was hoping for. "Are you telling me you mean to return, then?"

Fionn gazed worriedly back at her. "What else would I be saying? We are married, are we not? I shall be back again at midsummer. That is…if you'll still have me?"

Would she have him back? Well, of course she would. Aine opened her mouth to say so, then closed it again when she realized that perhaps, after all, she wasn't quite so sure. In another six months' time, it was very possible that the enchantment Fionn had woven about her could very well have dissipated. Perhaps she'd find out then that she'd never loved him at all. If that was the case, would she really want him back? If there was naught between them but enchantment, why take the risk? Why give him the chance to cast another spell and bewitch her all over again?

"I am sure all things will work out as they should." Kieran's words cut across the awkward silence. "And in the meantime, my liege, I wish you to know that I'm happy to stay on here, during your absence, to offer assistance to your good wife and explain things where I may."

"Stay?" Aine repeated, startled into speech. "Here? With me?"

No. It was impossible. Absolutely impossible. One magical creature in the household was enough—or quite possibly more than enough. She had yet to make up her mind about that.

She glared at Kieran in outrage. "You will do no such thing. I have no need of your assistance. Nor is it a boarding house I'm running. I'll not have it."

"No more will I," Fionn agreed. "I know not what you're up to, Kieran, but you keep your distance. She's mine. You're not to touch her. Nor interfere with her in any way."

"As if I ever would!" Kieran replied, scowling back at him. "Fate has decreed we two must share many things between us—crown and throne and even the same small copse—but never would I stoop to overstepping my bounds in such a way, nor take anything that was not offered me— freely and without duress. I have my faults, my liege, I'll not deny it. But that, I hope, has never been one of them."

Fionn snorted angrily. "Many things might seem to be offered freely, especially to one such as yourself. That does not mean you've any right to them."

"Indeed." Kieran arched an eyebrow meaningfully at him. "You'll get no argument from me on that point. That is something we'd both do well to keep in mind, as I've no doubt your good wife would agree."

"You leave her out of this," Fionn snapped. "I want your word you'll stay well away from here these next six months."

"That I cannot do." Kieran held up a hand when Fionn started to complain. "Stop. I have heard your objections, and yours, lady, as well, but I will not be moved. Given the conversation I interrupted with my arrival, I am surprised you'd even ask it of me. I will not leave my monarch unprotected, nor suffer any harm to come to him or to the woods in which he dwells, not if it be in my power to stop it. Not even though it means going against your wishes. I fear, my liege, that you've brought this trouble on yourself."

Aine's cheeks heated. Damn the man! How dare he sound so reasonable? How dare he seem to take her side, or take her husband to task for slighting her? How dare he use her own words—words she'd spoken in anger—against her? And, seeing as it was Fionn who'd provoked her in the first place and was therefore at the root of *all* her misfortunes, damn him as well. She was not "his" either, damn it. She belonged only to herself. And she'd thank both of them to remember that!

Who were these two men that they should presume to make decisions for her? She may have offered tribute to the Lords of the Forest in the past, but that was over with. If that was even who they were. In future they'd get naught from her that was neither an ax nor a blazing brand.

She was careful to keep *that* thought to herself, however, since it was clearly not in her best interests to say such things aloud, especially not while Kieran was anywhere within earshot. She'd learned that lesson quickly enough!

And, yet, if they were truly the godlike creatures they claimed to be, how could she hope to carry her point? A haze of angry tears obscured her vision as it occurred to her how futile was her outrage, how helpless she was against them.

She hated how powerless they made her feel. She hated the idea that she and Fionn must part in this fashion, with so much anger between them, with everything so unsettled. There was no time in which to resolve their differences, no time to make things right between them. If they ever could. If she even wanted that.

Most of all, perhaps, she hated that they could not even find one single moment of privacy in which to take their leave of one another. Everything was happening too fast. She'd had no time to come to terms with how she felt about any of it. All she wanted was a moment alone with her husband, a moment to think.

Maybe Kiernan could read her thoughts, for he cleared his throat before saying quietly, "Perhaps, if the lady does not object, I might step into the other room for a moment and leave you two alone?"

Aine nodded gratefully. But once she had the privacy she sought, she wasn't immediately sure what to do with it. The words she'd wanted to speak seemed to die on her tongue. How were they to say good-bye with this great distance already yawning between them?

"Six months," she said at last, speaking the words quietly, though how she did not know, for she wanted to wail her sorrow to the skies.

"Aye. Half the year."

Exactly as long as they'd been together. But whereas those months had seemed to fly, Aine was certain the months ahead would drag slowly, slowly by. "It will seem much longer, I fear."

"That it will," Fionn agreed sadly. "It will feel an endless, empty time without you. But my heart will be lighter and the days less dark if you will but tell me I might return to you at the end of it. Please, *a cuislĕ*. Give me that much hope at least."

With that, Aine's resolve broke, for how could she refuse to grant them both that single ray of hope? Nodding, she turned and threw herself into his arms with a shattered cry of "Yes." Only one sob was allowed to break from her lips. The rest she reined back, refusing to give in entirely to her grief, but nothing could stanch the flood of her tears. "Please come back to me, Fionn."

"Oh, Aine," Fionn muttered between kisses, "of course I will. *Is tú mo ghrá.* My dearest love, never doubt it."

A single moment, locked within each other's arms, was all they had. All too soon, Fionn was setting her aside, releasing her with a sad smile and a tender look in his eyes. He took a few steps away from her, heading toward the kitchen door, or so she thought, but he never made it that far. A great wind seemed to rise up between them, and it swept him from her sight. If she hadn't believed before that he was what he said he was, she had no choice but to do so now, for she'd blinked just once in surprise and in that same instant, he'd vanished, leaving only a handful of dry leaves behind to go scuttling around the kitchen floor in the wake of the mysterious wind.

Aine stared at them in horrified fascination, glancing up only when Kieran cleared his throat. There was a wary expression on his face as he gazed at her, coupled with sympathy and an unfathomable sadness.

"And what is it you want?" she asked. She was aware the question sounded churlish, but she didn't care. "As if ye have not yet caused enough trouble for one night."

"If I have, I am sorry. 'Twas not my intent. As to what I might want...I merely thought to inquire when supper might be ready?"

"Supper?" Aine repeated blankly.

Kieran motioned toward the unbaked loaves of bread she'd completely forgotten about. "Or tea. Or whatever you choose to call it. Your evening meal. I daresay you must be hungry after all this excitement. I know I am."

Aine shook her head. "Is it an inn you think I'm running? Don't talk to me of food. I'm sick at the very thought of eating. I've just lost my husband, in case you hadn't noticed—thanks to you and your interfering ways— and I've no appetite left to speak of. So you and your hunger may as well take yourselves elsewhere. To hell, perhaps."

"Don't speak nonsense, child. What have you lost? Why nothing at all. Your husband is merely off attending to business, as he's fain to be doing in any case at this time of year, with or without any 'interference' from me. And, furthermore, I'll have you know, 'tis a great honor he's been called to. So long as you do not do anything too foolish in his absence—like calling on yon woodsman, as you were threatening to do before—he'll be back at midsummer." His expression softening, he added, "You must eat, you know, for otherwise you will be wasting away in no time. Sure and young Fionn will be furious if that were to happen. If he were to come back and find you gaunt and famished he'll likely blame me."

"And he'd be well within his right to do so. Despite your protests, I am still not convinced you're *not* to blame for all of this."

Kieran smiled. "Some of it, perhaps, but surely not all. Now come, be a good lass. Put your bread in to bake and a kettle on for tea. Then come and sit down with me, and we'll have a talk."

"And what is it you wish to talk about?" Aine asked as she reluctantly set about getting supper started. "For I'm sure

I cannot think of anything we two might have to say to one another."

Kieran clapped a hand to his chest. "You wound me. Is there truly naught you wish to ask? I should have thought you'd be fairly bursting with questions."

Aine snorted. "Well, that shows how little you know me, doesn't it? For, as it happens, I've no interest in you at all."

"Is that so?" Kieran replied with a grin. "Well, never mind then. As luck would have it, I have more than enough questions for the both of us. So now, if you wouldn't mind, perhaps you might begin by telling me all about yourself and what you think of our lad Fionn."

"Oh, it's *our* Fionn, is it?" Aine all but snarled. If Kieran hoped to impress her by putting on airs and referring to himself in plural, he could think again. She would not be lorded over by anyone. Not in her own house, she wouldn't. "Sure and how exactly is he *yours*?"

Kieran's eyebrows rose. "Come now, can we not at least agree on that much? We each have a legitimate claim on him, surely. For all that he's your husband, lass, he's still my king."

Somewhat mollified, Aine nodded. "Aye. I suppose we might agree to that." Still, it struck her as strange that Kieran should feel a sense of fealty toward Fionn when it was clear he had the power to send him away against his will. "But, how is it you're both kings? After listening to the two of you tonight, I would have thought you were the more powerful."

A wistful smile curved Kieran's lips. "I suppose it may seem that way at times. But it is not really so. Our roles are complementary, you see. We each have strengths the other lacks. He is my king just as I am his. So it has always been, and so it shall ever be. And, as such, I have naught but love and admiration for him."

"Do you now? And does Fionn feel the same about you?" That was hardly the impression she had received.

Kieran's smile grew strained. "I couldn't say. Perhaps you should ask him?"

"Perhaps I would—an he were here. But as he is not, I'm asking you."

Kieran sighed. "Maybe not at this moment, but in time...he might yet learn to do so."

And in time, pigs might learn to fly, Aine thought, but she certainly wouldn't bet on it.

Chapter Eight

It took Aine several weeks to grow accustomed to Kieran's presence in her home, but it took Kieran even longer. Months passed before the question of *when* he might expect to feel her ax against his neck changed to *whether*. Before he found himself second guessing the assumptions he'd made and the actions he'd taken the previous year.

Though he'd made light of the effort, when speaking about it to Fionn, harnessing the power of the 'Tween to manipulate time was no small undertaking. But his fear for Fionn's safety, for his own safety, for the safety of their grove, had consumed the greater part of his common sense—much as a wildfire might consume the better part of a forest glen, leaving nothing behind but smoldering ash.

In his headlong rush to save his king, his people, everything he held dear, Kieran had spared no thought for the danger he himself was courting by following Fionn here. Then he'd further complicated matters by pledging to remain at Aine's side for the next half-year.

That, perhaps, was the most dangerous mistake of all.

"Explain something to me," Aine demanded one evening as they sat at her kitchen table, lingering over their tea. "You continue to claim you're not stronger or more powerful than Fionn, and yet when you speak of him, it's as though you were speaking of someone weaker or subordinate. Why is that?"

Kieran studied her in silence for a moment. The hint of accusation in her tone puzzled him. He knew—for she'd mentioned it often enough—that she still harbored feelings of resentment for the way in which Fionn had treated her, yet the look on her face said plain as plain that she would not stand for any slight to her husband.

She must really love him, after all.

The realization should have brought relief, but Kieran couldn't help but envy Fionn. What must it feel like, to be so loved? To have someone so firmly in your corner, ready to forgive your every transgression, willing to take on all comers in your defense, no matter the odds.

Even more to the point, what would Kieran not do to win a love like that for himself?

"Well?"

Kieran forced a smile. "Don't look at me so, lass. I assure you, I mean no disrespect. It's merely that Fionn is younger than I am, and is therefore less experienced. It's not a slight against him; 'tis simply the way things are."

"I do not understand that at all."

Kieran sighed. "Whether you understand it or not changes nothing. I assure you it's true. With age comes experience, perspective, some might even say wisdom."

Aine rolled her eyes. "Sure, and you must be daft, otherwise you'd know that's not what I meant; how is he young?"

"Well, he may not be, if you judge him by human standards, I suppose; but for a dru, he's practically a sapling. Whereas I, who you'd probably count as ancient, am still in my prime. There are many good years left in me, gods willing."

"But how is that possible? Since you're both immortal, are you not also ageless?"

"Immortal!" Kieran laughed out loud. "Oh, my dear, we're far from that. Is that what *he* told you?"

Aine's mouth thinned. "Fionn has had precious little to say about any of it. I'd just assumed. After all, you've both been worshipped since time immemorial, dying each year and being reborn. Are ye not gods?"

"That is in your mind alone. I've never claimed to be so, and I'll lay odds that Fionn never did either. As for the rest, surely by now you realize that all this talk of dying and being reborn is largely metaphorical? Legends are oftentimes based on truth, but you must not mistake them for the truth itself. There is, at any time, but one oak and one holly who bear the title king. Just as with your own kings, however, when one dies, another must take his place. We are tree spirits, for lack of a better term."

"Which means what, exactly?"

He smiled gently at her confusion. "It means we're as mortal as you yourself, for one thing. Other than that...we're each of us bound to a single tree. Its health is our health, its life our life. I can expect my tree to live as long as any other of its species. Or perhaps a little while longer, for very often it seems that being elevated to king results in a preternaturally long life, although that is certainly not always the case."

"And how long might that be?"

"For me? Three hundred years, perhaps; not so very long in the scheme of things. Fionn, on the other hand, will likely live a good deal longer. A thousand years, while it is in no ways common in this day and age, is not unheard of for an oak."

"A-a thousand?"

"It's possible, yes. Though, again, it's most unlikely. And while that may make us seem immortal to one such as yourself, I assure you we're anything but. Eventually we too will die, as all living things must do. Our trees will fall and decay and return to the earth, and our spirits will be absorbed back into the Forestmind from whence they came. Yet I prefer to think of this as a change from one state to another, a transformation, rather than an ending, and not so different from that which happens to us every year."

"Which is?"

Kieran shrugged. "Each year when the Oak King or I take up our crown, we give ourselves over to the life of the

Greenworld. Its strength becomes our own. Our consciousness expands, spreading outward through the Forestmind. It is...powerful beyond words, close to overwhelming. But this blessing is not without its price. Our sense of self is largely subsumed during that time, and it is oftentimes hard to find our way back to ordinary consciousness."

Aine eyed him for a moment without speaking, then asked, "And so after you there will be another Holly King—is that how it works?"

"Aye. 'Tis how it has always worked, and how it always will. When I am gone, another will take my place. Mind you, I am in no great hurry to speed that process along. Nor I'll wager is young Fionn. I'll thank you to remember that."

"And is death the only way you can be released from this service? Can you not abdicate your throne aforetime and let another take your place while you are yet alive?"

"You cannot be serious?" Kieran stared at her in surprise. "Do you honestly think, if Fionn had been free to choose last December, that he would not have chosen to stay with you?"

"Why not, if it's such an honor?"

"It is, but it's not one he asked for; no more than I did. Nor was it possible for either of us to refuse. Once the title was conferred upon us, there could be no going back. It is unalterable. We are what we are, and so we remain."

"But how are such things decided? Neither of you have children to pass your crown on to, do you? Or siblings? Or parents from whom you inherited them?"

Kieran shook his head. "You're thinking too much like a human; we are not the same. While we don't have families as you know them, we do very often develop a fondness for those in our home grove. Although that, I suppose, is more a matter of proximity and familiarity than anything else. In any event, the kingship is not something that belongs to any of us by birthright. It cannot be passed on or passed down or given away to anyone else. The choosing is a mystery. When a new king is needed, the Lord and Lady bestow the crown upon whomever they judge best suited for the role, but make no mistake, 'tis a burden as well as an honor. It requires sacrifice, the giving up of everything we are, everything we hold dear, for months at a time."

"It sounds lonely."

"Aye. 'Tis often a very lonely thing we are called upon to do, even for such solitary creatures as ourselves. And that is another reason, or so I have always held, why there must be two kings, belonging to each other, partnered for life, as it were. Why else would we be granted several days at the turning of each cycle in which to commune with one another? It is not just to share the burden—nor less the honor—but to share the loneliness, and so, perhaps, to halve it."

"It almost sounds like... No, never mind." A faint blush colored Aine's cheeks. "I've no idea what I'm saying. It's a daft idea."

Kieran stared at her curiously, intrigued by her blush. "Please, go on. It almost sounds like what?"

"Well, this partnership you speak of, it sounds very like what a marriage is—or what it should be. Almost as though the two of you...as though you were...mated. To each other, that is."

He could not help but smile. "That's very perceptive. Sometimes, that is *exactly* how it is. After all, there is naught to stop us, when we take on physical form, from mating just as humans do. We can and we do. And I do not mean with mortal women like yourself—that, in fact, is most unusual. In general, we find it better to stick to our own kind."

He broke off then, laughing at the indignant expression on Aine's face. "Oh, now, do not look so shocked! Are you a child that you should claim to be unaware of such things? Why, it was you yourself who brought it up! Tell me, why should we not find comfort in each other's arms or take pleasure with our other halves?"

The color on Aine's face deepened. She shook her head. "You misunderstand me. It's not that I object to what you've said, at least in theory. It wouldn't concern me at all, except...well, where does that leave me? That's what I'd like to know. Is this a game to Fionn? For, if so, it seems a cruel one. He promised himself to me in marriage. I did not ask him to do so—it was his idea! By what right did he tie me to him when he already had a...a partnership with you?"

"I have no idea what he was thinking," Kieran replied, surprised by the bitterness in his own tone. "Not about any of it. My first thought last summer was that he had gone entirely mad. But, as for my relationship with Fionn, I assure you there is naught that need concern you. We are not on intimate terms. Nor is it likely we will ever be so again. So you may rest easy; whatever else he's thinking, I'm sure he means to keep his vows to you."

Aine's eyes narrowed. "Again? So you *were* intimate at one time? Is that what you're saying?"

Kieran sighed. "Aye—once. But what we had does not even warrant a discussion. It was as brief as it was insignificant—a mistake on my part, a lapse in judgment on his, an aberration that I'm sure we've both long regretted."

"Tell me about it anyway," Aine said. "I would know more about this...lapse."

Kieran opened his mouth to refuse her and found that he could not. Perhaps he'd been waiting for a chance to tell his story. Perhaps it would ease his pain to speak of it; for it was certain that staying silent had never helped. "It happened long ago by your reckoning, on an exceptionally beautiful day in the midst of the most beautiful summer you ever did see. But no, I am lying already. It was not even a day. It was no more than an instant, a single drop in the ocean of time, a single flower plucked from a field of daisies..."

Kieran could still recall with crystalline clarity every detail of that long ago encounter and the young man with whom he'd shared it. The very beautiful young man whose hazel eyes had gazed at him so adoringly, who'd come to him so willingly, and who'd shaken his soul so profoundly that even now, years later, he could not think back on that interlude without regret for the way he'd ended it. Cruel, Rory had called him, at the time, and Kieran could not disagree. Cruel and foolish and shortsighted.

Fionn had been little more than a means to an end. A beautiful, willing, and eager means, to be sure, but nothing more than that. He was young, impressionable, biddable, and altogether gorgeous. In short, he was absolutely perfect for Kieran's purposes.

And yet...why then, when Rory had understandably expressed an interest in Fionn, had Kieran felt so unaccountably dismayed? Wasn't that precisely what he'd been counting on?

"More. More. Give me more," Fionn had begged as Kieran knelt behind him, spreading the boy's taut buttocks, laving his tight hole, readying him... *"Do it now. Please."*

Even all these years later, Kieran's cock still swelled as he recalled the sound of Fionn's pleas. Oh, how he'd enjoyed hearing them; how he'd deliberately taken his time just to make him cry out again and again. He remembered too how it had felt to be buried within that strangling heat, how Fionn's body, warm, pliant, damp with sweat, had shuddered and arched beneath him.

And then it was over, and silence settled around them as they sagged together against Rory's tree. A silence that was broken only by birdsong and their own shattered breathing. A silence that went on for, perhaps, a little too long.

Maybe Fionn had been waiting for Kieran to say something, or maybe they'd both been too wrung out for conversation. For his own part, Kieran was already regretting his impulse.

For, as it turned out, having Fionn had done nothing to ease Kieran's need for Rory. It hadn't left him feeling satisfied, or justified, or pleased with himself. In fact, it had made him feel worse, oddly empty, strangely conflicted for reasons he could not fathom. Fionn was certainly not the first lover Kieran had taken, nor the last. But there was something memorable about him, something that refused to let Kieran be.

Afterward, Kieran tried to tell himself it was only his imagination playing tricks. Surely there was nothing amiss. The silence was likely neither as long nor as awkward as he'd imagined. For that matter, so what if it had been a trifle lengthy? It had been a companionable silence, surely, and there'd been no need for either of them to break it. Kieran tried hard to convince himself that they'd both gotten everything they'd hoped for or expected from the encounter—everything they'd wanted, everything they'd needed.

He'd tried his best to rewrite events, to erase the memory of hurt and dejection on a young man's face. Because afterward...oh, afterward, that had been when Kieran had made an even worse and bigger mistake. Not only had he sent the younger man away without so much as a parting kiss, but the following spring, when Fionn had shyly approached him, Kieran had dismissed the younger man out of hand. He'd barely even glanced at him. He certainly hadn't been civil.

A means to an end, that's all Fionn had been—so Kieran had told himself again and again. And once he'd served his purpose, Kieran had gone out of his way to make it very clear to the lad that he had no further use for him.

Aye, that had definitely been a mistake...

"An aberration?" Aine repeated skeptically. "Is that so?"

Kieran nodded. "Clever lad, I think he realized straightaway he wanted nothing more to do with the likes of me. Since that time he has shown not the slightest interest in renewing our acquaintance. So you see, my dear, 'tis nothing you need worry about."

"So then...was it your relationship with his predecessor to which you referred earlier? Did you know the previous Oak King?"

Kieran bit back a sigh. The enormity of his loss still stung, as it probably always would. "His name was Rory. Rory Tighearnach. You should know and use it with respect, if you intend to speak with me about him, for I would not have him be forgotten."

"Tell me," Aine prompted.

"Ah, where do I start?" Kieran mused. "The first thing one noticed was his presence. A more majestic creature, the world will never know. He was older than I, and never once did he let me forget that fact. Indeed, he loved nothing better than to tease me about my youth, my inexperience, and many other subjects besides. His was a sunny, jovial spirit, warm and expansive, dominant when it suited him, and at other times patient as time itself. He was the very model of restraint. And a very good thing he was too, for if you can imagine, I was once even more reckless than young Fionn. But Rory was always there for me, to lend an ear if ever I needed to talk. We leaned upon each other's strengths, we shouldered each other's burdens. Most of all, during those few hours that were given us to be together, we were lovers. In short, we were everything to one another." He paused, no longer certain that was the case. "Or maybe it just seemed that way. Who am I to speak for him? There may have been others in his life more important to him than I. What I do know to be true, however, is that he was everything to me."

"I see." Aine gazed at him hesitantly, then asked, "What happened to him?"

It was a logical question, Kieran supposed, but still, it caught him off guard. He fixed Aine with a searching stare. If she'd been asking out of idle curiosity or ghoulish fascination, he would not have answered, but her eyes held only sympathy and concern, reminding him that she, too, had known loss—and far more recently.

"He died—more proof, if still you need it, that we are *not* immortal. His tree was struck by lightning during a freak spring storm and very nearly cleaved in two. A grievous injury, it left his heartwood exposed and vulnerable to the elements so that when the *Foehn* wind arose, a short while later, it desiccated him from inside out, before ever the sap had a chance to rise. Had it happened during the dark half of the year, I'm almost certain he would have healed, for he was still quite hale. If he could not have done so by himself, I would have bent all the power of the Greenworld to the task. As it was, however, his spirit remained scattered all across the breadth of the Forestmind, like leaves tossed by the wind. He never returned to himself, or to me. By the time I took the throne, by the time I sent my own spirit off in search of his, every trace of him had quite faded away. I never heard even the faintest whisper, at least nothing that I could identify as such. He seemed not to be anywhere within the Greenworld. He was simply...gone."

A heavy silence fell between them. Once again, the memories arose, so thick and deep that Kieran thought for sure they'd drown him, thought he'd suffocate from the weight of his loss as it pressed upon his heart. It would be a blessing, in a way, if he did; an escape from the pain that ran so deep and sharp, that still seemed so fresh...

"I am sorry." Aine sounded stricken as she reached across the table to grasp his hand. That touch, the first caring contact he'd had with another living creature in oh, so long, undid him. "I am most truly sorry. I did not mean to cause you pain."

Tears rolled down Kieran's face unheeded. He felt his heart crack open once again. Long moments passed before he could answer. "You did not. 'Twas not you who caused me pain. I just... I never thought I would have to live without him, you see. 'Twas not the way it should have been. Oaks live longer than hollys—much longer, as a rule. That's the way of it; it's how it's always been. Even though he was older, I should have gone first. I should have had him with me to the end."

Aine said nothing. She continued to hold his hand, offering silent comfort, until he'd recovered himself. Only then did she resume speaking with an air of great casualness, as though nothing untoward had occurred.

"And so Fionn… I assume 'twas he who took Rory's place? Is that the way of it?"

Kieran sighed. "Indeed it was." He shook his head as he thought of it. "As unlikely as it sounds, it was Fionn the Lord and Lady chose to be king in Rory's stead. And a greater shock I still cannot imagine as that which I felt when first I learned of it. It was truly the last thing I'd been expecting."

Aine stiffened and pulled away. "Oh? And why was that? Did you not think him qualified?"

"Qualified? No. Of course I did not. Were you not listening? I judged *no one* fit to take Rory's place."

"I see." Aine glared at him, bristling once more as she came to Fionn's defense. "So then, since, by your own words, no one could meet your impossible standards, why should Fionn *not* have been given the honor? The task had to fall to someone, did it not? Why not choose him?"

"Oh, no, good woman." Kieran smiled sadly. "You will get no argument from me on that account. Indeed, I fear you misunderstand me. I cared not who was chosen. Where in the world was there an oak who could equal Rory? Nowhere. Such a one did not exist. But, Fionn… A young tree from my own grove, someone who'd grown up under my very nose, as it were, someone I'd hardly even deigned to notice, more than a time or two. Someone I'd…" *Someone I'd treated so badly.*

"It did not sit well with you. I see. So you hold it against him. Is that the way of it?"

"Calm yourself, lass. I do not say any of this to speak ill of him. He was just so young, so green and untried—and brash, as the young are ever wont to be. We have butted heads a few times over the years. Even now, as you have no doubt observed, things are not easy between us."

"Aye. I had noticed that."

"I suppose, if I am to be completely honest, I *did* think him an odd choice for the role at first. I may even have resented him for a time. But for him to be singled out for so great an honor at so young an age must surely be a testament to his quality and his worth. I am confident he may yet become a most extraordinary king. Always assuming I can keep his wife from taking her ax to him whene'er he chances to annoy her," he added teasingly. "Not that she would not have my sympathy were she to be so murderously inclined."

An angry flush colored Aine's cheeks. "I have no interest in your sympathy. And Fionn has no need for you concern. So you may keep both to yourself. You must know by now that I never *truly* intended to do him harm. I was just angry, as who would not be? Not three months wed, and he informs me that he must leave me? And then the tale he weaves to explain his actions is so far-fetched that even a child would think to question it. Even now, I..." Her voice trailed off, and she fixed Kieran with a narrow-eyed glare. "Even now, it seems to me I've seen little enough proof that either of ye are truly what you say ye are. How do I know you have not made this all up between ye?"

Kieran nodded. "And that, no doubt, is exactly why he put off telling you for as long as he did. Why interrupt a pleasant idyll with the unpleasant truth, especially if you are not even going to be believed?" The excoriating scowl on her face had him raising a hand to forestall her protests. "Now, now, I'm not offering excuses for the man. I agree he should have told you long before he did. But you must admit he had a point. What proof could he have given you that you'd have believed? Did you not think it passing strange when you saw him spring up before you in the forest?"

"I certainly should have done so," Aine replied angrily. She got up abruptly and began to clear away their plates. "But the morning was so uncommonly misty, and... Perhaps it's some form of druish magic. He cast a spell upon me— that's clearly the way of it. Obviously we're well-suited after all, Fionn and I. You must think us *both* mad, I suppose— him for marrying, and me for believing he loved me. And perhaps you are right. Perhaps we are."

"Aine." Kieran reached out and snared her wrist when she would have hurried past him. "Wait." They both stilled. In the shocked silence that followed, Kieran was hit first by the realization that this was very possibly the first time he'd spoken her name aloud and next by the soul-deep conviction that no name had ever sounded more fair, nor felt more right upon his tongue. He slid his hand down until it was clasping hers. "Aine," he repeated again, more softly this time and for no other reason than the pleasure it brought. "I apologize, *a leanbh*. My dearest child, I should not have teased you as I did. This world is filled with mysteries, great and small, but Fionn wanting to marry you is not any one of them. His love for you is so clear to see no one could ever doubt it. And the same is true of your feelings for him."

"Is it?" Sorrow clouded her eyes.

Kieran nodded. "If you would know the truth, I envy you both for what you have found."

"And what is it I have found then? Who is to say it is even real? Perhaps I am in love with him or perhaps, as I've said, I have merely fallen under a cruel spell."

"Or perhaps there is not as much difference between the two states as you seem to think? Love *is* magical—never doubt it. Indeed, it is the greatest spell of all. I was there, you know, on that morning when he first appeared to you. I remember thinking at the time that I'd never seen him look more beautiful than he did in that moment, standing before you, naked and vulnerable. Fearful though I was for his safety, I could not help but admire him and wish that I possessed even a fraction of his bravery. I don't know that I've *ever* had the courage to go after something I wanted in so bold a fashion. If, in his eagerness to win your heart, he erred in his treatment of you, then let me offer my apologies on his behalf. We're none of us without fault. And I would never call *anyone* mad for loving too well."

Aine scowled. "Now who's the liar? You already did. Do you not remember it? 'Twas only a handful of minutes ago."

"Did I?" Kieran sighed. "Aye. I suppose I may have done so. 'Tis not the first time my tongue has tripped me up—of that you may be certain. But will you not forgive a bitter old man a moment of foolishness?"

The real question was could Kieran forgive himself? He'd chosen to seal himself away with his grief and his pride and to ignore his feelings for Fionn for far too long. He could see now where that had taken him, how much time he'd wasted, how much joy he'd sacrificed over the years. Aye, and how much pain he'd likely inflicted as well. For surely no one behaved as Fionn had done unless he'd been driven to it.

Kieran's new awareness was forcing him to recognize his own foolishness, his own stubbornness and pride. His own deeply buried desires.

Who could say what would have happened if he'd acted differently? He should have made his desires and intentions plain. He should have found the courage to apologize decades ago! He hadn't. Now, he had no business feeling resentful over how things had turned out. Neither Fionn nor Aine were to blame for any of it.

"You are not so old," Aine protested. "Or so I've been given to understand. Still in your prime, was that not what you said?"

"Are you attempting to flatter me, lass?"

"Hardly. I am merely repeating your own words back to you. It's you who said it."

"I believe you're right again. But, in truth, dear lady, you deserve at least some of the credit for that, or the blame, however it might be. Why, with you I feel almost a child again."

Aine snorted. "Now who's the flatterer?"

Kieran smiled. "Guilty as charged." Driven by fear, he was certainly behaving as foolishly as a child—quick to action, slow of thought, too hasty with both his words and his deeds.

He had made up his mind that he would answer all Aine's questions, tell her everything she wanted to know, anything she needed to hear, if it might help to keep her from cutting down his grove, but he'd never stopped to think what such a course might do to him. It had been so long since he'd spoken about these things to anyone, much less to so pure and gentle a spirit. He'd failed to take his own feelings into account. He hadn't realized how all his unspoken thoughts had piled up inside, precariously balanced, but far from stable.

Like a single pebble might start the landslide that would take down an entire mountain, so it had been with him. Once he'd started talking, once he'd begun giving voice to his grief, to his memories and regrets, he found it difficult to stop, even though every word, every revelation, every memory he uncovered was another callused layer that he'd had to peel away from his too raw, still aching heart.

* * * *

Over the next several months, as Aine came to know Kieran better, she was pleasantly surprised to discover he was not as cold and unfeeling as she'd initially thought him. Dour his mien may have been at times, yet she sensed a dark, seductive warmth smoldering deep within, needing only a spark to bring it to light. It called to something wild within her, something that yearned to be that spark, to be the one to set his heart ablaze.

Like a roaring fire on a bleak and bitter night, there was something about him that made her want to draw close, far too close for safety's sake; that tempted her to curl up naked beside him and dare his heat to sear her skin. Only it wasn't just her skin she risked by getting too close to Kieran's fire, but her heart as well.

By the first of May the tension between them, and within her heart, had begun to wear on Aine's nerves. She was tired of the raised eyebrows she encountered every time she met one of her neighbors, tired of having to make up stories to explain Fionn's absence and Kieran's presence in her home.

Tired of the lies. It was Kieran who first dreamed up, and later promulgated, the unlikely pretense that he and Fionn were brothers.

"You'll forgive my saying so, but I don't see a resemblance." If Aine had heard that once, she'd heard it a dozen times over. "Why, the two of you are as different as night and day!"

And each time, Kieran would respond with equanimity and an impish gleam in his eyes, either cheerfully claiming it was something he and Fionn had been hearing their whole lives, or sadly confiding that indeed he wished he could be more like his brother.

"You're a shocking liar, do you know that?" Aine groused as they returned home from shopping in the village, their arms laden with bundles. It was a beautiful spring day. New life was burgeoning all around them. It was the kind of day that should have gladdened her heart. Instead the sight of all those green and growing things brought Fionn to mind and all the foolish dreams and wishes she'd entertained the previous summer.

Kieran's green eyes danced with mischief as he shot a mocking glance her way. "And are you just now discovering this about me? Who was it you thought you were honoring with your prayers and your pretty songs when you came into the woods to pay homage to the Holly King?"

Aine's temper flared at the reminder. Her religion, once such a comfort to her, was now a sore point. Though she'd never acknowledged the fact, meeting Fionn and Kieran had called all her beliefs into question. She should have felt validated, yet all she knew was loss. Since December she'd been eschewing all the rituals that had once brought her solace and peace. "What I thought of you when you were but an ideal to me is neither here nor there. It annoys me to see my friends and neighbors being played for fools."

Kieran shrugged. "What is it you want me to say to them then? Surely you don't expect me to tell them the truth?"

"Of course I don't. But, all the same, must you take such pleasure in deceiving them?"

A dimple appeared in Kieran's cheek as he smiled. "I confess it does amuse me. But why should I not derive what pleasure I can from such things? As Lord of Misrule, it's a part of my duties. I am obliged to play the trickster whene'er possible and set conventions on their heads. But it's all in good fun, is it not? Who am I hurting?"

Aine firmed her lips and said nothing. In truth, she did not know how to answer that. In his own way, Kieran was every bit as compelling as Fionn, especially when he flashed that particular smile. But whereas Fionn was like sunlight and green grassy fields—filling her heart with joy and making her want to sing and dance and make love for days on end—Kieran's pull on her emotions was more subtle and perhaps more dangerous. She did not entirely trust herself where he was concerned.

"Come, you must have known something of my nature beforehand," Kieran pleaded. "This cannot have come as a complete surprise?"

He sounded so lonely. Despite the sunlight, warm against her skin, the soft desolation in Kieran's voice left Aine chilled. "There are times when I question whether I know anything about anything."

"I know there is that about me which is twisted and dark," Kieran continued in earnest tones. "I have never denied it. But I am what I am, and whether you choose to believe me or not, I do regret that my presence here has disrupted your ordered world. Perhaps such disruption is necessary at times. All new life begins in chaos, does it not?"

Aine sighed. "You may be right, I suppose." Despite her best intentions, she could no more harden her heart against him than she could spread her arms and fly to the sun. "And despite what you say, I doubt you're as dark and twisted as you pretend."

Again the dimple appeared. Kieran's eyes lit up. "Ah, but as we've just discussed, you hardly know me. You have no idea how dark my tastes may run or what twisted desires I might be harboring."

Aine stopped in her tracks, caught between dread and anticipation. "Perhaps you should tell me about them?"

Kieran stared back at her, his eyes heavy-lidded and dark. "Perhaps I should show you instead?"

Before Aine could think of a reply, Kieran had dropped the packages he'd been carrying and was reaching for the ones in her arms as well.

"Here now, what are you doing?" she asked as her bundles joined his on the grass by the side of the road. Instead of answering, he glanced up and down the empty road, then stepped close and caged her face in his hands. Aine froze. She stood unmoving as Kieran's lips touched hers. He tasted different than Fionn—that was the first thing she noticed. He tasted darker, spicier, yet equally tantalizing.

Kieran crowded closer. He tilted her head to the side, then slid one hand into her hair to anchor her there. When the pressure of his fingers tightening on her scalp made her moan, he quickly took advantage and slid his tongue into her open mouth. Then he wrapped his other arm around her and pulled her so tight against him Aine could scarcely catch her breath.

Heat flared between them and continued to build until, finally, she kissed him back. Her mouth opened wider to allow his probing tongue better access, and her hands found their way to Kieran's waist without any conscious thought at all. His body felt hot to her touch. Hard and strong. Better than she could ever have imagined, but different, somehow, than what she'd been expecting. He was a different size, a different shape. He wasn't Fionn.

The thought of her husband broke the spell. Aine wrenched her mouth free and pushed at Kieran's chest. "Stop."

He did so at once, letting her go and stepping away with a look of dismay on his guilt-stricken face. "Aine…"

"We cannot do this. I've made promises! We both—"

"I know! I know. I'm sorry. It will not happen again. I give you my word."

He'd said exactly what she wanted to hear. So why was she as disappointed as she was relieved? Why did her traitorous body continue to clamor for more? Aine smiled at him sadly. "And is your word worth anything, O king?"

Kieran glanced away, shamefaced. "It used to be."

"Then I'm sure we'll be all right," she said as she bent and began to pick her packages back up. "Now, come. We need to be getting home."

* * * *

They never made reference to the matter again. Kieran was ever the gentleman after that day, always at pains to put her at her ease. He kept a careful distance between them, as though that could stop the thoughts from running wild in Aine's head!

If anything, the distance made things worse. She could not stop thinking about it. Often she'd find herself absently touching her fingers to her lips as she recalled every detail, the press of his mouth on hers, the warmth of his breath, the taste of his tongue.

And she couldn't help but wonder, what if it had not ended there? What if they'd climbed the wall that edged the road and lain together in the grass where no one would have seen them? What would it have been like to make love with Kieran? How would he have differed from Fionn? What would it be like to have them both at once?

As spring turned into summer and the solstice drew near, these were the thoughts that kept her company each night as she lay all alone in her bed, missing Fionn, longing for Kieran, stroking her own flesh, toying with her nipples, and bringing herself to ecstasy again and again.

Chapter Nine

June 1895
At the time of the summer solstice

Dawn was still but a suggestion hovering below the horizon when Kieran closed the cottage door behind him. He stood for a moment, taking deep breaths of the cool, clover-scented air, wishing he could hold back the day just a little while longer. He hated to leave with the future so uncertain. Would he be back in December...or ever again? *Should* he come back? And what sort of greeting might he expect if he did?

But all those questions would have to wait until the proper season; he'd get no answers today. He'd taken just a few steps along the path that led to the garden gate, when the door behind him was flung open once again.

"Kieran, wait!"

He turned in surprise, breath catching in his throat at the sight of Aine as she came flying down the path, her red hair streaming out behind her. His smile felt shaky as he greeted her with false cheer. "You're up early. Anxious to be reunited with your husband, I presume?"

Aine did not return his smile. "You're leaving." The hurt in her voice was mirrored in her eyes. "Without even saying good-bye?"

"Aine." Kieran reached for her automatically, only managing to stop himself at the last moment. "What's all this? I thought we had said our good-byes last night?"

She wrapped her shawl more tightly around herself and looked away. "No. No, that wasn't good-bye."

"My dear..." What more did she want from him?

She shrugged. "It feels...strange not to be going with you, not to be on my way to the grove this morning. I should be there."

Kieran's heart clenched at the thought. "We discussed this." And he really couldn't stand to argue the point again. He couldn't have her there. "We agreed."

Aine's lips tightened. "No, *you* discussed it; and made up your mind for both of us."

"Please." He clasped her hand and squeezed it tight. "Don't fight me on this. Trust me."

"I do trust you," she replied, eyes wide with surprise as she turned her gaze to his once again. "What has that to do with anything?"

He didn't answer—because, really, what more was there to say? She stared at him for a moment longer, worrying her lower lip, her expression irresolute. Perhaps she was waiting for him to change his mind, but he could not.

Finally she sighed. "Very well. If you insist. Until December, then?"

Now it was Kieran who hesitated. He should demur. Spend another season with her like this last one? Tie himself in knots once again until it felt as though he couldn't breathe? He didn't know if he could bear it.

He should cut things off between them now, quick and clean, while he was still able to, before he made another terrible mistake. But maybe some mistakes were inevitable? And, after all, he'd made this particular mistake—the mistake of walking away too soon—once already. He might as well try for something new. In the end, he raised her hand to his lips and pressed a gentle kiss to her knuckles. "Of course, my dear. December."

* * * *

Fionn had begun the agonizing process of wrenching himself free of his tree as soon as enough of his mind had coalesced. It was easier now that he had a reason to want to leave his post, but the change still left him tired and disoriented. Even so, he gave himself no chance to rest, but immediately launched himself at the veil. He stumbled a bit as he pushed through it, so that he landed on his knees on the cushioning moss. As he struggled to his feet, panting from exertion and shivering slightly in the misty morning air, he scanned his surroundings feverishly.

His eager anticipation quickly gave way to dismay as a lone figure appeared from out of the fog. Fionn's heart all but froze in his chest at the sight.

"Where is Aine?" he demanded, scowling at Kieran as fear hardened his heart.

"She awaits you at home," Kieran replied evenly. With a small flourish, he magicked a set of clothes—wool trousers and a linen shirt, from the looks of it, similar to those he was wearing. Bowing slightly, he presented them to Fionn. "If I may?"

Fionn made no move to take them. "Why?"

Kieran straightened, smiling sadly. "Why do I offer you clothing? Why not? It is but a small courtesy. I thought you might find them useful and hoped to spare you the trouble of manifesting them for yourself. I know how exhausting it can be to expend so much magical energy all at once. And it occurred to me you might prefer to reserve what energy remains, so that you might expend it later in…other activities."

"No," Fionn corrected. "Aine. Why is she not here?"

"Ah." Kieran laid the clothes upon a nearby boulder. "That is also my doing, I fear. I judged it likely she would prefer a measure of privacy in the event you wished to indulge in the aforementioned activities sooner rather than later." He paused, and when Fionn offered no response, he added in helpful tones, "Your wife is most anxious to be reunited with you."

His wife. Tears clogged Fionn's throat. He reached out, almost blindly, for the clothes Kieran had provided and quickly began to dress. He felt vulnerable enough as it was, begging Kieran for information, for reassurance, with his need so obvious and his emotions clear on his face. He did not need to be naked before him as well. Still, he could not quite trust the relief welling up in his heart. Possibly because he knew he did not deserve Aine's forgiveness. Possibly because he could not believe she wouldn't have fallen for Kieran, just as he had. Six months. What he wouldn't have given, once, to have so long a time to spend with the Holly King. He paused to shoot a sharp glance in Kieran's direction. "Was there any other reason she chose not to meet me here?"

Kieran sighed. The sound was so unexpectedly mournful it caught Fionn off guard. Was it possible Kieran had tried to seduce Aine and failed?

When Kieran spoke, however, his words were not what Fionn expected. "I thought it might distress her to see you at such a time. We are not always at our best, are we, when first released from service?"

Fionn had to bite his lip to keep from answering. That was a half-truth, if ever he'd heard one. He'd seen Kieran, and Rory too, for that matter, immediately after leaving their trees. They exhibited no discomfort, no loss of energy, no weakness—nothing, in short, to cause anyone distress. It was only he who was so afflicted, so graceless and inept. This could only be a kindness on Kieran's part. Fionn was not quite sure what to make of that. "How is she?"

The haunted look left Kieran's eyes at the question; instead, his face lit up with pleasure. "She is quite well and, as I said, very eager to see you again. You should make haste."

"I intend to." Averting his gaze again, Fionn suited his actions to his words. The smile on Kieran's face, the warmth of his tone, only added to Fionn's confusion. What had transpired here over these past six months? What surprises were still in store for him?

He couldn't decide how he was feeling at the moment, or even how he *should* be feeling. He was grateful to Kieran for his kindness and consideration—if that was truly what was motivating him. But what if it was something else? What if there was something more, some dark, unpleasant truth that Kieran was neglecting to tell him? Should he be thanking him, or demanding more information?

Suddenly aware of the silence that had stretched between them, Fionn glanced up sharply. His gaze collided with Kieran's and surprised a small, sad smile on the Holly King's face, a look very different from the one he had worn only a moment earlier. Whatever it was, it was gone in a flash.

Before Fionn could get a word out, Kieran had spread his arms wide and called the wind to him. His clothes went first, disappearing in a cloud of petals and leaves as the breeze rose up and surrounded him, and then he himself was gone. Fionn inhaled sharply as the sudden dip in temperature raised gooseflesh on his arms and legs. His throat felt full, and he nearly choked on the smoky scent of dry leaves. The sharpness stung his eyes and touched a melancholy chord within his heart. He felt a pang of loss.

Perhaps Kieran had not outright lied to him, but how much of the story might he have left out? Perhaps Aine had stayed home in part to spare Fionn from seeing her grief at losing Kieran. Would that grief outweigh her joy at being reunited with him? There was only one way to find out.

Fionn's doubts accompanied him all the way back to her cottage, slowing his steps. But Aine must have been waiting for him in the garden, because she came running out to meet him as soon as he came in view of the house.

Her eyes were bright with tears as she launched herself at him. "Oh, Fionn," she sobbed. "You've come back. You've come back to me at last!"

"Aine." Fionn caught his wife around the waist and hoisted her into the air before kissing her soundly.

She was gasping for breath when she wrenched her mouth free. She wrapped her arms around his neck and buried her face against him. "I have missed you so!"

"And I, you," he said as he squeezed her even more tightly, wanting never to let her go again. "My love. My only love."

FIONN'S WORDS DREW another sharp sob from Aine. His only love? Ah, if that were true, then she was indeed the most wretched of women.

Her distress did not go unnoticed. Fionn pulled back to gaze worriedly at her. "What's wrong, a mhuirnín? Why all these tears? What's troubling you?"

"What troubles me?" Aine made an effort to rein in her emotions but was not entirely successful. Her voice sounded shaky, and when she tried to smile, her lips still trembled. "How can you ask such a thing? How could I not be overcome with joy to have you back again after so much time apart?"

For all that it was true, Aine felt a pang of guilt, as she recalled their conversation the previous December. When she'd accused Fionn of lying to her, and he'd countered by saying he'd merely suppressed a part of the truth, she had not been impressed with his logic. Yet here she was now, doing the very same thing.

Fionn lowered her to the ground, and set her on her feet. His eyes were wary as they studied her. "It seems to me there's more to it than that. I see as much grief in your expression as I do joy. Are you certain that's all that's amiss?"

Aine shrugged helplessly. "How am I to answer that? Six months is not an inconsiderable time to be parted— especially so soon after being wed. Still, I suppose you are right. There may be more that's been wearing on me than just the time apart. There's the entirety of this strange new life you've plunged me into. It was not of my choosing, after all. And to have it sprung upon me as suddenly as it was…"

"You need not remind me," Fionn replied, sighing heavily. "I know I've wronged ye, but I was desperate and did not know what else to do. At the time…I was a fool. I was hoping the winds wouldn't find me here, hoping you'd never have to know. I didn't want to lose you!"

"You haven't lost me, Fionn." Aine framed his face tenderly. This time when she smiled her lips felt less tremulous. "And you're in no danger of doing so. Nor need you fear my temper. I believe I convinced even Kieran to trust me by the end. So there's no need for you to hide my ax."

Fionn's mouth tightened. "Kieran." Something flashed in his eyes, though it was gone again before Aine could decide what it was. Hurt, perhaps. Or fear. Or bitterness. "Is he a part of what's grieving you, then? You didn't have any trouble with him, did you?"

"Trouble? No. At least not in the way I think you mean that. He behaved in a perfectly gentlemanlike manner."

Fionn's gaze searched her face, his eyes wary and uncertain. "But he has troubled you in some other way. Is that what you're saying?"

Aine shook her head. "No, Fionn. I'm saying nothing of the sort. It was a shock at first to have him here, but that was months ago. We've long since made our peace with one another."

Another half-truth. There was nothing "peaceful" about her feelings for Kieran. Indeed thoughts of him continued to trouble her even now. In the past few weeks she'd been forced to confront her feelings and admit to herself how dear he'd become to her, and how reluctant she was to see him go. Not that she'd spoken of this with Kieran, of course. Out of loyalty to Fionn, she'd kept her feelings to herself. As had he. Not a word had Kieran spoken about his feelings for her, even though she suspected that he'd come to care for her as well. Certainly nothing else could account for the rigid courtesy he maintained after their kiss, or the yearning she'd spied in his gaze each time he'd looked at her.

Which was not to say she'd come to prefer him over Fionn. That wasn't the case at all! Why, she'd been as anxious as ever for her husband's return. No, the truth was far stranger and more complicated than that. She'd fallen in love with them both.

On second thought, why should anyone think that strange? They were a pair, the two of them bound to each other, and now to her. Why should they *not* both be in her heart? And no matter how wrong it might seem, or how unlikely it was to ever happen, why should she *not* wish to have them both in her bed as well? But that was not a conversation for today.

Instead, she took hold of her husband's hand. "Come inside now," she urged. "You must be famished. Let me make you breakfast, as I did last year."

An eager light gleamed in Fionn's eyes. "Our first meal together! I remember it well. And can you promise me that today's breakfast will end in much the same manner as last year's did?"

Aine felt her cheeks flame. "Indeed, I feel very confident that will be the case, and there is nothing that would make me happier."

* * * *

And so summer passed once again in a bliss-filled haze—at least for the most part. Fionn seemed at times more heartsore than before. And Aine didn't have it in her to grieve him further by giving voice to her own confusion, to her doubts and uncertainties, to her newfound desires, so she did her best to put them from her mind. Still there was no use denying or attempting to ignore how much her life had changed.

Where only a year before, Aine had had no man in her life, nor wanted any, now she had two, in a manner of speaking. Both of them so bound to their duty and so constricted in their own freedom that they impinged hardly at all upon hers. As autumn advanced, she found herself growing resigned to her strange new fate—even if she did worry once in a while about what the future would bring or how they would make this very odd situation work out for all three of them. Things had changed—aye. But maybe not as much as they all needed them to.

She had one other cause for worry as well, and a far more pressing one. As the days continued to shorten and the world turned its face toward winter, Aine more than once observed Fionn eyeing Kieran's tree with a look on his face she could not interpret. Dark and indecisive, at times it made her think she might not be the only one who was struggling with issues of desire and temptation. At other times, however, it made her wonder whether she shouldn't hurry and hide her ax.

Chapter Ten

December 1895
At the time of the winter solstice

From his vantage point, beside the farmyard gate, Kieran surveyed the seemingly peaceful scene spread out before him. The night was still with nary a breeze to stir in even the topmost branches of the nearby trees. High above his head, thin white clouds stretched misty ribbons across the sky, blotting out great swaths of stars and wrapping the half-dark moon in a gauzy embrace. Kieran studied the orb's shadowed form for several moments, the better to divine her wishes. Fionn might claim to serve the sun alone, but Kieran, Ruler of the Waning Year and creature of the 'Tween, knew better. There was naught on this earth could escape the Night Queen's influence.

In a little over a week, when the moon rose full, it would be for the thirteenth time this year. A rare and unusual occurrence, it signaled a time of transition and change, a time when one might reasonably hope to alter one's path. A hot swell of anticipation arose within him as he thought of it, the moon of opportunity and rebirth. The opportunity to change—wasn't that exactly what he needed, what they all needed?

Tonight. Why should it not be tonight?

The sentinels of the forest were used to biding their time. A delay of several decades before a goal could materialize or a dream come to fruition meant little to one such as he. That didn't mean he didn't suffer through the waiting, however. It didn't mean he couldn't yearn, or covet, or long for what he could not have, what he might never have, or what he might have foolishly thrown away.

Tonight. Please let it be tonight.

On the surface, the cozy farmhouse nestled in its tidy yard looked much as it had the previous year, snug, warm, and inviting, but as Kieran well knew, looks were oftentimes deceiving.

Last year, even despite the pleasant setting, the sight of this place had sparked only fear and uncertainty within him. Tonight, the small stone building, with its whitewashed walls and slate-tiled roof, with candles burning in the windows and a lazy curl of smoke eddying from the chimney, marked the seat of all his hopes and dreams, as well as the crux of his restless discontent. Within its four walls resided everything he longed for and ached to possess.

It was that which kept him standing out here in the cold, which made him hesitate, afraid to enter or even to make his presence known to those inside. Fear. Anticipation. Hope. Uncertainty. Excitement. Desire. Love. Regret.

If his dreams were ever to be realized, it would have to happen sometime. It might be now, or a hundred years from now. Kieran would much prefer it be now, of course, but even a hundred years was better than the third possibility— that his dreams should die aborning and never be realized at all.

Maybe he'd already had his chance and lost it. Maybe what he longed for now would never be his again. In truth, he didn't know what to expect. That, at least, was the same as last year.

He'd sped here last winter on the full moon's bright wings and his own breathless terror, his whole mind focused on a single goal—that of saving Fionn's life. When he'd arrived at the farmhouse, it was just in time to hear Aine's threat to cut down his grove—and out of nothing more than spite! It had seemed to Kieran then that his fears had all been justified.

Now, he could laugh about it. A smile creased his face as he remembered it. How fierce and fiery she'd appeared. Despite the danger she'd represented, she'd been radiant with her red-gold hair catching the fire's light and her blue eyes gleaming like sapphires over her flushed cheeks. Even smudged with flour and seething with rage, she'd been a sight to render him almost speechless.

She'd seemed even more magnificent in her anger and wounded pride than she had on that previous midsummer morning. She'd looked like a goddess or a proud young queen as she'd stared Fionn down. Her hands had been fisted on her hips. Her chest had heaved with every angry breath. But queens and goddesses are ofttimes cruel, as Kieran was well aware. And, in that moment, nothing about the situation had struck him as even remotely humorous.

On the surface, his plan to stay close and keep an eye on his temperamental goddess had seemed a good one. He'd thought it sensible, rational, certainly harmless enough. It turned out, of course, to be anything but. How could he have known how disastrous it would prove to be? How could he have ever anticipated that, in the process of getting to know Aine, he would fall so deeply in love?

The fact that she was Fionn's bride should have been his strongest ward against her. That alone should have sufficed to keep his feelings in check. He'd been insulted when Fionn suggested he might be planning to seduce his wife. In retrospect he could better understand the Oak King's concerns.

On the other hand, Kieran would dare anyone to do what he had done—spend six months in Aine's presence, day in and day out—and not fall under her spell. Over the course of those six months, he'd become hopelessly enthralled. And when it came time to leave her, the grief had nearly killed him.

Last summer, he'd told himself he was only acting to protect Fionn when he convinced Aine to wait at home for her husband to return, rather than venturing out into the woods to meet him there. And it was true in its way; it didn't hurt Fionn to have a moment to himself. Mostly, however, Kieran had been protecting himself.

The hint of despair in Aine's eyes as he bid her good-bye had done more to warm his heart than even a thousand summer days could have achieved. It was that memory he wanted to take with him into the darkness. It was that he wished to hold on to during his months away, not her subsequent joy at being reunited with her husband.

And tonight, it was that memory that finally propelled Kieran to push open the farmyard gate, that and the hope of what he might see in those eyes tonight, if he were lucky—his own feelings reflected back at him.

Chapter Eleven

Fionn had been dozing by the fire, with Aine in his arms, when the knock came at the door. He started awake, a single thought in his head. *Kieran.* A bucket of ice water upended over his head could not have woken him up more thoroughly. *No! Too soon! Too soon!* It was all he could do to keep from groaning aloud.

A puzzled frown furrowed Aine's brow. "Who could that be? Someone other than *him*, surely? Else, why would they knock?"

Fionn tightened his arms around her. "I neither know who it is nor care why they're knocking. It could be him, I suppose. It would be just like him, to keep us guessing." He'd long since given up trying to determine what the Holly King would or would not do in any situation. As to why he might choose to do it? Ah, well, one may as well waste time wondering what made the wind to blow, or the sun to shine. Kieran was a mystery, a force of nature, as darkly intriguing as he was unfathomable. Such had been the case for as long as Fionn could remember. He very much suspected Kieran liked it that way.

The knock came again, longer and louder, and this time Fionn did groan at the sound. "Damn the man! It must be him." Anyone else would have had the decency to go away by now.

Aine gazed at Fionn questioningly. "Shall I answer it?"

Fionn shrugged. "If it pleases you to do so. What care I? Do as you will."

"Thank you for that." Aine shot him an exasperated glare as she pushed herself out of his arms and got to her feet. As she headed across the room, Fionn let his eyes fall closed in despair.

"So it is you," Aine's voice cut through the silence. Though her tongue was sharp and her words coolly mocking, something in her tone turned the curt greeting into a caress.

"Waiting on ceremony, Your Majesty? Since when is it *you* bother knocking? I thought such simple courtesies were merely for us common folk?"

"Aine. How good it is to see you again."

If honey had a voice, it would sound just like Kieran; it was not the first time Fionn had thought so. Now, he gritted his teeth as the soft, sweet tones sparked both jealousy and desire, weighing on his chest until he almost couldn't breathe. He clambered to his feet, then turned to face his nemesis. "You're early. Again."

"That I am." Kieran's eyes rose to meet Fionn's. A lazy, hopeful smile had curved the Holly King's lips. "But since 'tis only by hours this year, rather than days, I hope I'll be forgiven for the intrusion?"

"Hours or days, it matters not," Fionn growled. "'Tis still early."

An almost wistful look replaced Kieran's smile. "Indeed. And I beg your pardon. I'm not here to displace you yet, my liege, nor hurry your departure. I merely thought that, since we both were freed of our duties for the moment, you might allow me to pass the time here with you and your wife. 'Tis but one evening only. Might I not trespass on your hospitality for that long?"

"It's Aine's house," Fionn replied stiffly, his emotions too conflicted to sort out. "'Tis for her to decide."

Kieran inclined his head. "Of course." He turned his smile on Aine. "Well, Mistress O'Dair? What say ye?"

Aine cocked her head to the side. With her back to Fionn, he couldn't see her expression. Was she returning Kieran's smile, or favoring him with a regal look of disdain? Had she furrowed her brow or narrowed her eyes as she struggled to make her decision? Or were those sky-colored orbs twinkling with amusement in that way he loved? He held his breath while he waited to see what she'd say. When she finally answered, however, it was in a voice that was neither sunny nor cool nor gave any indication what she was feeling.

"Why don't you go and sit by the fire and warm yourself?" Aine gestured toward the hearth. "I'll put on some tea." Fionn subsided back into his chair. In truth, he did not know himself whether he was relieved or disappointed by Aine's response. He trained his gaze on the fire once again and pretended not to notice when Kieran seated himself in the other chair.

"I trust I find you well?" Kieran asked, after a moment had passed in awkward silence.

"As well as can be expected." The churlish sound of his own voice grated in Fionn's ears and left him wanting to cringe. In an attempt to salvage the moment, he added a belated, "And you?"

"I am also well. I thank you for asking."

Fionn chanced a quick glance in the Holly King's direction. At this close range, Kieran's eyes seemed dark and endless, mesmerizing. As their gazes tangled, panic tightened in Fionn's chest. His mind scrambled for distance, for safety. He wrenched his gaze away while he still could, before he was caught and all his secrets laid bare. He stared moodily at the floor. "Why are you *really* here?"

Kieran hesitated. "The truth?"

He sounded so taken aback, Fionn couldn't help but laugh. "Aye. Why not? 'Twould be a novelty for you, at the very least."

"I fear you may be right in that." Kieran sighed. "Very well then. I've been thinking about your wife."

"Oh, indeed?" Anger churned in Fionn's gut as he raised his gaze to glare at the other man. "Have ye now? And why is that?"

"What I was wondering is…do you think it fair that she should have to forgo, for six months each year, all the attention so beautiful a woman might reasonably expect to receive from her husband?"

Guilt washed over Fionn. Of course it wasn't fair! He'd long since come to the realization that *nothing* about the situation in which he'd placed Aine was ever going to be fair.

"It is what it is. Fair or not, I can do nothing about it at this late stage."

Again Kieran hesitated, giving Fionn the impression he was choosing his words with care. "Perhaps it is not something you need deal with on your own. If I may...perhaps I could be of service. To you both."

"Service, is it now?" It was all Fionn could do to keep from smirking. Perhaps Kieran had not chosen his words so carefully after all. Fionn could think of more than one way in which the term could be applied. "Tell me, *my liege*, what kind of *service* is it you wish to offer? And to which of us?"

"If you could give me leave to...well, to court her, for lack of a better word."

"To...court her?"

"I know you'd likely prefer to keep her to yourself, as who would not, but since you cannot be here for so much of the year, could we not both share the task of caring for her? Assuming she's willing, of course."

Shock stilled Fionn's heart for a second. He could not have heard Kieran aright. Recovering, he slammed his hand down on the arm of his chair. "Aine would never—" He broke off abruptly. In truth, he had no idea what Aine would think of such a plan. His mind insisted on replaying all the conversations he'd had with her over the past six months regarding Kieran. He saw again the flush that lit her cheeks, the dreamy look on her face, the hint of guilt in her downcast eyes. Not that he blamed her. He knew as well as anyone how hard it was to resist the Holly King's charm, how damn nigh impossible.

Damn and blast. Maybe she *would* want that after all.

"She would never play you false," Kieran agreed, finishing Fionn's sentence for him, although the words he chose were not the same as Fionn would have done. "That goes without saying. Nor would I, for that matter, though I do not expect you to believe me. That is not at all what I'm suggesting."

"Is it not?" Fionn asked absently, paying barely any mind to Kieran's words. He was so lost in the new series of images unfolding in his mind. Aine and himself. Aine and Kieran. The three of them together, Aine coming undone for them both. And then he and Kieran... No. Impossible.

"This is why I came here tonight," Kieran continued. "Rather than to wait until tomorrow. I needed to talk to you. I wanted to give us a chance to explore the possibilities, to give *you* a chance to...well, to consider whether or not you're willing. A chance, perhaps, to show your wife that you are truly open to whate'er will make her happy, rather than merely telling her that you are. I thought she might put more faith in actions than in words."

Fionn scowled. "Are you suggesting she cannot take me at my word?"

"No, no. Of course not. I'm sure she has every confidence in you."

Fionn pursed his lips. He, on the other hand, was not so sure of that. "So you've come to cheat me out of my last night with her—is that it? You wish to bed her tonight, while I do...what exactly? Stand idly by in order to somehow prove my supposed willingness to allow the two of you to continue on in this same manner for the whole of the next six months? Well, I've no need to consider *that* for very long. I can give you my answer now. I won't stand for it."

"No, no," Kieran said in alarm. "You misunderstand me. I promise you that's not at all what I was proposing."

"It makes no difference to me what you're proposing," Fionn insisted, trying desperately to ignore all the impossible thoughts clamoring for his attention. "Whatever it is you're suggesting, I've no interest in it. Sell it someplace else, if you can. There must be someone who'll listen to you—naive, idiotic youngsters looking to be taken advantage of. Sure and the woods have always been full of them. Is that not so, my liege?"

"Fionn..."

"'Tis Aine's house," Fionn repeated stubbornly. "I've said it once already tonight. 'Tis her life and her bed as well. It is for her to decide for herself who she wants in any of them. And if it so happens that's you, either during the months I'm gone or altogether, so be it. I'll not deny her right to choose. But if you're asking me to be happy about it, you're asking too much."

Kieran sighed. "Forgive me. It was never my intention to upset you. I assure you I would never seek to keep you from your wife or displace you from your own bed, nor in any other way cause you distress. I thought we three might...possibly...work something out between us."

"Work something out? The three of us? Ah, sure and you're daft." And I'm a coward, Fionn thought miserably. A coward who couldn't even contemplate the possibility; it was too overwhelming. Once in each year already he had to cede his place to Kieran, to withdraw his mind from the Greenworld and relinquish his throne. That by itself was more than enough. As Kieran had reminded him last summer, Fionn still didn't know how to do so without disgracing himself. His own weakness terrified him.

"If you're inalterably opposed to the idea, you need simply say the word," Kieran said quietly. "I promise you'll hear no more about it from me. All I ask, however, is that you give it some thought before you decide. 'Tis a lonely life we're called to lead, you and I. And while I can well understand your desire to take a wife—to have someone you might share even half the year with, it seems cruel to ask her to also share in our loneliness. Not when it's so easily remedied."

"Easy?" Fionn fairly shouted the word. "What's so bloody easy about it? There's nothing easy about any part of what you're suggesting!"

"Fionn. May I speak to you for a moment?" Aine called from the pantry door.

Fionn's heart sank. If she'd merely gone to the pantry to fetch some tea, she'd been about it a surprisingly long time. She must have heard every word they'd said. He ground his teeth in impotent fury. He could only imagine what she wanted to speak to him about. Why must every parting between them be so deucedly hard, so unendingly complicated? "Now you've done it," he muttered, shooting Kieran a murderous look at as he got to his feet.

Aine was pacing anxiously when Fionn joined her in the small pantry. "Well, what is it?" he asked as he folded his arms and leaned his shoulder against the doorjamb. He regarded his wife warily. Her cheeks were flushed, but her expression gave little away.

"I couldn't help but overhear your conversation," she began.

Fionn nodded. "I feared as much. And? Are you scandalized by the scoundrel's suggestions?" he asked hopefully. "Are you sorry now you didn't turn him away when you had the chance?"

Aine bit her lip. "No, not exactly. Though, I'll admit, what he proposed did come as a surprise."

"I should hope so," he replied, feeling miserable. "And a lesson to me, that was. Ne'er again will I ask him for the truth."

"Are you so sure it's the whole truth you heard from him tonight?" she asked tentatively. "It's not that I'm calling him a liar, mind you, but I think there may be parts he's left out."

"Such as?"

"Well, for one thing, I noticed that while you and he both have had a great deal to say about me—your feelings for me, your desire, your concern—you haven't said much about what the two of you might want from one another."

"What we want?" Fionn shook his head. "All I want is for him to leave us alone!"

"Do you really?"

"Aine..."

"I think the reason Kieran's here tonight is as much for you as it is for me. Perhaps more so, since the two of you have so much less time to spend together. To put it plainly, I think it's *you* he wants. And, unless I miss my guess, I think you want him as well."

Fionn straightened away from the door frame. "I've no idea what you're talking about. The idea is preposterous. I want *you*. I chose *you*. 'Tis you I married—as you yourself reminded me not so long ago."

Aine sighed. "I know." She reached out for him and drew him close. He went willingly into her arms, his hands spanning her waist. "I remember every word I said last night, and every word you had to say last year, on the same subject. And I believe you. But my love, will you not be honest with yourself—and with me? Can you honestly tell me you feel nothing for him?"

Fionn could not. But neither would he admit to his feelings, or give her the words she so clearly wanted to hear.

Aine cuddled closer, her breasts flattening against his chest as she reached up to wrap her arms around his neck. "Will you not at least promise to entertain the suggestion I'm about to make and not dismiss it out of hand?"

Fionn tightened his grip on her waist. "I'll consider whatever suggestion you care to make. But can you not send him away in the meantime? We've yet a few hours to spend together, you and I. I do not wish to waste it."

"No, Fionn." She rested her head against his shoulder. "He cannot leave, for that would defeat the purpose of what I'm about to suggest to you."

"I'm listening."

"What I'd like, or rather, what I think would be best— and this is just for tonight, you understand, it need not be for more than that, if it displeases you."

"Go on."

"I think we should take him into our bed."

"Into our bed?" Fionn held her away from him. "You cannot be serious?"

"Indeed, I am. This matter has been hanging over us both for some time now, whether you choose to admit it or not. And I do not wish to go through another year wondering how we are to work things out between us. Nor do I wish *you* to go through the next six months fearful about what might be happening here in your absence." She smiled sadly at him. "And I know you. I know how it will prey upon your mind, how you will doubt yourself. It grieves me to think of it."

"Are you so sure it's *me* you're thinking about?" Fionn asked sadly. "Perhaps, after all, you find you *are* sorry that you're not married to him?"

Aine's smile turned teasing. "Nay, *mo chroi.* My dearest husband, never think it. For, if that were the case, what influence would I have to wield over you now that would make you do as I wish? 'Tis much better thus. Will you not indulge me in this, husband? 'Tis *my* last night with *you* too, after all. Should I not get some say in how it's to be spent?"

"You've made it quite clear to me how you wish to spend it. You wish to spend it with *him.*"

"No, I wish to spend it with you both. Do not pretend to misunderstand me, Fionn, or pretend it's something you've never thought about. Kieran's told me something about your past together, you know."

"Aye. I can see he's told you *something*, all right. Some fairy tale no doubt, from the sound of it. Why is this so important to you?"

"Because of what I sense from you both. I thought last year that it might be the case, and now I'm sure of it. Even when you're apart I can feel it, a yearning, a sadness, an unmet need, but it's stronger when you're together."

Fionn swallowed hard. "I know not what you mean. I feel nothing of the sort."

"There's a bond between you—or at least, I feel there ought to be. Instead, there's a distance there, and it feels all wrong to me. There's an emptiness inside him, and I think it's because of you."

"An emptiness? Inside of Kieran?" Fionn snorted. "Sure and that would be his heart, lass. Or, rather, the absence of it."

"I think he's lonely."

"Lonely!" Fionn shouted in outrage. Why should all her sympathy be for Kieran? Had she none for him?

"Not so loud, my love."

Fionn struggled to lower his voice. "Aye, very likely you're right. No doubt he *is* lonely—as am I, for much of the year. And what am I to do about that?"

"I would like you to help him," she replied stubbornly.

"Why?"

"Because I'm asking you to. And because I think it might help you as well. It's what I want tonight, what I *need* from you."

"I see." Fionn glanced away, his jaw clenching, his heart sinking with guilt. "And I suppose you think I owe you that—as penance for my actions last year. Is that it?"

Aine sighed. "Well, maybe I do think that. Would I not be within my rights? But I promise you, love, I am thinking of you as well. You need this as much as I do, Fionn. We both need to know that what we have cannot be broken. I do not wish to have this issue—to have Kieran—come between us any longer," she said, stopping suddenly, as though she were listening to the words she'd just said. A wicked smile curved her lips. "Well, on second thought, maybe in a way I do wish that, but only for the sake of giving pleasure to us all."

Fionn shook his head, refusing to be either amused or aroused by her words. "I don't see how this would benefit any of us. You don't know him, lass. Not as I do."

It didn't even matter that what she was offering him now was everything his younger, more carefree self might have wished for. That younger self no longer existed. Fionn was king now. He had responsibilities. Unfortunately, he also had responsibilities to his wife.

He knew he'd acted badly last year. He'd been foolish and reckless, and this was the result. Marry in haste, repent at leisure—was that not something humans said? He'd never heard the saying before last year, but now he wished he would have, because it seemed that was just what he'd done. He'd rushed Aine into marriage, kept too many secrets from her, and now...now they'd both had plenty of leisure in which to repent.

The obvious attraction between Kieran and Aine had been making him crazy for months. His own attraction to them both—aye, that made him crazier still. Knowing he'd be leaving soon, that he'd be leaving the two of them here together, all on their own for the next six months? That might be the thing that made him craziest of all—Aine was certainly right about that. Especially since, for all those very same months he'd be alone. Alone and likely worrying himself into distraction wondering whether there'd be anything for him to come home to at the end of that time.

So he'd do whatever he could to make her happy, anything that was in his power to do. He'd even share their bed with Kieran, if that was what she wanted. And, apparently, it was *exactly* what she wanted.

Chapter Twelve

Tonight Aine would not go to the woods to celebrate the solstice, as she had in years past. Tonight the woods had come to her.

That thought was uppermost in her mind as she lit candles in her bedroom. Just as they'd done earlier, when she'd lit the candles in her parlor windows, the words to her solstice prayers echoed in her mind. A part of her was still shocked by the course this night was taking, by her own boldness and the men's agreement—Fionn reluctantly, Kieran even more quietly, but with such a look of eager gratitude gleaming in his eyes that she wondered how it was she'd ever thought him cold.

Underlying the shock, however, was a sense of surety. It felt almost inevitable. Even before she knew them, even before she understood that the oak and holly kings existed anywhere outside the realm of legend, she'd loved them—not just one of them, but both.

She'd loved their strength and their honor, their willingness to sacrifice themselves for the good of the world. But that was the ideal of them. The men themselves were not without their flaws, but then again, who was?

They strove to live up to that ideal, however, and that surely was the more important thing. And when they gave themselves—to an idea, to a person, to a goal—they gave themselves fully. A year and a half was time enough for her to have learned that about them. And what more could one ask for in a lover? In a hero? In a god?

"Is this not what you pray for when you make your ceremonies?" Kieran had suggested months earlier. *"To commune with your gods? For them to appear to you in human guise?"*

"And are you a god, then?" Aine had asked, smiling in response, mocking his attempts at solemnity. *"Is that what you're saying now?"*

Kieran had snorted at that, his laughter laced with derision. *"I told you already that's not the case. We're creatures of earth and spirit. We're no different at all from you in that respect. And if anyone tells you otherwise, he's a liar."*

"Are you sure this is really what you want, a mhuirnín?" Fionn asked now as he wrapped his arms around her from behind. He pulled her close and laid his cheek against her hair.

Was he hoping she'd say no? Or was he merely seeking to reassure them both? A tremor ran through her, excitement warring with unease. She had to swallow hard before she could answer. "Aye."

She leaned back against him, resting for a moment in the comfortable familiarity of his arms. His erection prodded against her lower back—and that too was a comfort. For all his reluctance, it was clear he wanted this too. Emboldened, she nodded. "I do. I really want this, Fionn."

Fionn sighed. Disappointment? Acceptance? Relief? Aine didn't know what it signified. Maybe he didn't know either, maybe there was no easy or obvious answer to the question. She made no protest as he turned them both around, so they were facing the room. So that she was facing Kieran.

The Holly King's eyes were hot upon her, his desire plain to read. As he stalked toward her, erasing the distance between them, she felt her heart speed up. She wondered if Fionn could feel it too.

Kieran leaned in and cupped her face in his hand. When he brushed his lips against hers, it was more a promise than an actual kiss, sweet and soft, questing. As he moved to straighten up again, she rose up on her toes to follow him, wordlessly demanding more. More of his taste, more of his mouth, more of him.

Kieran's eyes widened. For an instant, she thought he might push her away. Instead, he drew a quick, startled breath and leaned in again, eyes blazing. This time, his touch was sure and possessive. He clasped the back of her head in a firm grip. Canting his head to the side, he kissed her harder, moving in a half-step closer, until she felt herself sandwiched between the two men. She'd rested her hands on Fionn's arm where it banded around her waist. Now she lifted one to reach for Kieran, skimming her fingers over his chest, using a soft, exploratory touch to learn his contours. His build was leaner, his hair more wiry than Fionn's, his muscles more sinewy. Her mind was so busy cataloging all the little differences between the two men she almost missed the moment when Kieran lifted his head to meet Fionn's gaze.

"Undress her for me?"

It was an order, a request, a plea... Perhaps even a test of sorts? Once again, Aine was not quite sure. The undercurrents of emotion that flowed between the two men were dark, hidden, like a subterranean stream. But all the same, identical shudders racked both her body and Fionn's. Awareness. Heat. Eager need. *Yes.* Aine allowed herself a small, triumphant smile. *He does want this. He needs this too.*

Kieran's hands dropped to his side as he took a step back. His eyes were trained on Fionn's hands as they moved to undo the button at the neck of Aine's shift. She reached back with both hands to clasp Fionn's thighs. She needed the touch to anchor herself. She needed to draw on his strength because her knees were threatening to buckle under the weight of Kieran's gaze. She watched his eyes move, their focus shifting from Fionn's face to hers, back again, then sliding down the length of her body, following the slow, steady progress of Fionn's hands on her buttons—neck, to chest, to waist. Her shift gaped open, nipples hardening at the inrush of cool air over them. Then Fionn moved his hands to her shoulders and skimmed the garment down over her arms. Fabric pooled at her wrists and waist.

She shivered in the sudden draft, aching for the touch of Fionn's hands, until Kieran closed the gap between them. Kieran filled his hands with her breasts, holding them gently at first, almost reverently, as though he were satisfied just to learn the feel and the weight of them while he kissed her again. Then he pulled back to look at her. He shifted his hands so that his thumbs could stroke slow circles around her nipples.

"I remember these," he murmured, staring at her in seeming fascination. "From midsummers past. I wanted to touch them like this then."

Aine shivered in response, remembering that morning a year and a half ago. The cool moss beneath her legs, the quiet trill of birdsong, the melancholy hush—had it been Kieran's sorrow she'd felt in the air that morning, or Fionn's? Then as now, she wanted to erase that sadness. She wanted to conjure up heat and light and celebrate the solstice by banishing everything dark or cold or empty.

Kieran's fingers closed around the swollen tips, tugging and rolling them, until he'd forced another needy cry from her throat. "I thought you so beautiful then," he murmured. "So brave, so lovely, so enchanting. But you're even more so now."

Aine pressed closer to Kieran. She freed her arms from the bunched-up shift and let the garment drift to the floor. She was trembling in earnest now, almost painfully aware of her own nakedness, aware of the two men surrounding her, almost dwarfing her with their height, exactly as she'd imagined it...

No, not exactly. This was far, far better than she ever could have dreamed. The smell and the taste and the heat of them, the sound of their breathing filling the air— she hadn't imagined any of that. She'd never thought about the way Kieran's moustache would tickle against her skin as he bent to take one ripe nipple in his mouth. She'd never expected that Fionn would press against her from behind, fitting his hands to her waist and lifting her so that Kieran need not bend so much. Or that Kieran would slide his hands beneath her bottom, supporting her weight as he sucked even harder. She hadn't imagined how she would writhe between them, almost dancing in place, so frustrated by her need to have them both at once.

She wanted to wrap herself around them both, wanted to split herself in two so she could touch them both as they were touching her. So she could kiss the two of them, taste the two of them, feel them both inside her.

Fionn bent his head and nibbled at her neck and shoulder. She was startled when she felt his cock push between her thighs to ride her cleft, hot and slick and demanding. She shifted her hips back automatically, wanting more, wanting him inside her, but even as she did, she was aware of a sense of confusion and loss. When had he opened his pants? He must have taken his hands from her long enough to undo the fastenings, to pull his cock free. How had she failed to notice any of that? How had she missed seeing him, feeling him, touching him? So much was happening—and all at once, it seemed. She wanted to pay attention, catalog every detail, burn it all into her memory...but she couldn't split her focus to that extent. Already, there was so much she was missing.

Why had she ever suggested to Fionn that she might want this for one night only? One night was never going to be enough. She should have known that from the start.

The head of Fionn's cock slid across Aine's clit; the thick rim bumping against it sent a jolt of need to her core. She spread her legs wider, whimpering for more. She wanted to taste him on her tongue, *needed* to taste him—now. She was on the verge of pushing Kieran away, brushing all their hands aside so she could turn and kneel and take Fionn in her mouth when Kieran's teeth closed gently on her nipple, recapturing her attention and startling another needy cry from her throat. She surged forward again, rocking back and forth, faster and faster now as her hunger grew, as a clawing need for more, more, more built inexorably within her.

Fionn straightened abruptly. Reaching over her shoulder, he laid a hand against Kieran's shoulder and pushed. Kieran raised his head. His eyes, heavy-lidded, glazed with heat, searched out Fionn's face. His gaze was questioning, doubtful, faintly pleading. Aine felt a momentary annoyance with both of them—for stopping, for leaving her dazed and bereft, for communicating wordlessly with each other and not with her.

This was not just between the two of them, however much they might think otherwise. There were three of them in this room tonight, and they each deserved a say in what went on here.

"Fionn," she murmured in protest, even as he swung her up into his arms. "What are you doing?"

"Need you, a mhuirnín," he said, his eyes hot on her face as he carried her toward the bed. "I can't wait any longer. Need to be inside you. Now."

Ah. Yes. That. Aine nodded. "I want that too." Then turned her head and buried her face against his neck, clutching him tighter as a wave of heat swept over her. It was all so right, yet it was almost too much. She felt herself in danger of being overwhelmed by their concerted attention.

Fionn placed her gently on the bed and then came down beside her. She hadn't been mistaken, she realized now. Somewhere along the line he'd managed to divest himself of all his clothing. How or when that had happened, she had no idea. Perhaps it was magic?

Fionn tugged her close with one big hand splayed across her midriff and spooned her against him. He slid his other hand into her hair and pulled her head back so he could kiss her neck. She closed her eyes for an instant, almost dissolving in bliss.

Kieran took a moment to shed his own clothes before following them down—no magic for him, she supposed, which frankly surprised her. He'd always struck her as the more mysterious of the two men, perhaps even the less human. As he settled himself next to Aine, however, she sensed nothing strange or mysterious or unusual at all. He was so beautifully naked, so divinely wrought, so quintessentially male. In the dim light of the candle she'd lit earlier, his muscles were clearly delineated. A smattering of dark hair marked his chest, and his cock, at least as long as Fionn's, though not as thick, was rigidly erect, bobbing against his abdomen.

Kieran lay on his side, just beyond Aine's reach, with his head propped on his hand, as he watched her watch him. No, she quickly corrected herself; it wasn't her he watched but *them*. If Aine had still harbored any doubts as to which of them Kieran really wanted this evening, the look in his eyes would have laid those doubts to rest. He wanted them both—the two of them at once. She knew and recognized that need, felt the kinship between them. She still wasn't sure if Fionn understood why she needed this tonight, but Kieran did. She knew that without either of them having had to say a single word.

Though Kieran hadn't so much as touched Fionn once all evening, that look on his face told her everything she needed to know about his feelings for the younger man. The yearning expression in his eyes gave away all his secrets.

Aine was far less sure what Fionn wanted, however. Perhaps he did a better job of burying his emotions. Perhaps he really *wasn't* interested in Kieran in the same way. Privately, she doubted it. The tension between the two men was palpable. It was silent and unacknowledged and perhaps all the more potent because of that.

She reached out a hand to draw Kieran to her, wanting him closer, needing him to be a participant in this, not merely an observer. As Kieran slid closer, once again erasing the distance between them, Fionn slipped his hand beneath Aine's upper thigh. He lifted her leg, maneuvering her so that her thigh came to rest on top of Kieran's hip.

She shuddered at the contact. For an instant, her entire attention was captured, focused right there on the sensitive skin of her inner thigh, on the warm-skin-over-unrelenting-bone that was Kieran's hip, on the heat and the slide of their bodies against one another, the unfamiliar rasp of his hairy thigh against her smooth one.

Then Kieran's hand settled at her waist. Their lips met in a quick and scorching kiss. Fionn pressed his lips against her shoulder from behind, and she was once again aware of being sandwiched between two hard, muscular bodies, of being the fulcrum on which the other two depended, the needle of their compass...or was it they who were the spinning needle to her due north?

Fionn snuggled in closer, pushing her forward just enough to make her even more intimately aware of her proximity to Kieran, of his heat and his strength. Of his arousal. Kieran's cock brushed against her abdomen, the tip sticky and wet, prompting her to hook her foot behind his leg and rub herself against him. The muscles of his abdomen rippled in response. He groaned softly, then lowered his head and pressed his lips to hers in another tender kiss.

Fionn's actions were not purely altruistic, however, as Aine quickly realized. This new position, in which he'd placed her, left her wide open to his touch—a fact he clearly intended to take full advantage of. He slid his hand between her legs and trailed his fingers up and back along the length of her slick crevice several times, before finally burying one finger inside her. She moaned in pleasure, rocking her hips back against him, wanting more.

"You're so hot and wet now, aren't you?" Fionn murmured. "So ready for my cock. So ready for me to fill you."

So, so ready. Aine was beyond speech. She tried to nod, but Fionn's hand was still fisted in her hair, holding her immobile. She sucked in a quick breath as the realization of her own vulnerability hit her. How easy it would be for either of them to completely curtail her movements, to position her however they liked, to do with her whatever they wished. Which was exactly what she wanted, but no less overwhelming. They were her gods, and she was their tribute; she wanted to give them everything. But even more, she wanted them to demand everything from her. Her eyes fluttered closed as she sank into the bliss of surrender, reveling once again in the feeling of being surrounded by them both, of being the center of their attention, of being exactly where she wanted and needed to be.

"Answer him." It was Kieran's voice that whispered in her ear, startling her into opening her eyes once again.

She looked at him in confusion, having already forgotten the question.

"Tell him what you want." Kieran's words were an order, a seductive threat, accompanied by a sharp tug to one nipple—for emphasis. Speech became even more of an impossibility.

"Aye." Her voice sounded thick and sluggish as she struggled to shape it into words. "Aye, Fionn. Now. Please."

"A mhuirnín," Fionn growled softly. "Take me, then." He dropped a quick kiss on her shoulder and took hold of her buttock, holding her open, steadying himself, anchoring them together. "I'm all yours, Aine," he said as he thrust inside her. "Always yours. Forever."

Forever and ever, Aine promised silently as she arched against him. She caught his rhythm right away and was soon rocking in tandem with him. Her eyes slid shut again.

"No." Kieran cupped her face, forcing her attention outward once again. "Open your eyes. Let me see what he does to you."

"It's what you're *both* doing to me," Aine corrected, as she met that glittering, needy gaze. *And what we're both going to do to you before this night is over*. She slid a hand between their bodies and took hold of Kieran's cock, loving the feel of the heavy shaft as it pulsed and kicked within her grasp. She stroked along its length a time or two, then paused to run her thumb over the plump crown.

Kieran groaned. Rocking his hips, he forced more of his cock through the tight ring of Aine's fingers, dragging precum over her hand when he withdrew.

Ah, what she wouldn't do for a taste of him. Aine was tempted to bring her hand to her mouth and suck the silky fluid from her fingers, but that would have to wait. For right now, it was enough for her to bring him along and make sure he knew he was a part of this, a part of them.

A rosy flush swept up his chest. "Need to touch you too," Kieran said as he slipped a hand between Aine's legs. He found her clit and began to fondle the little nub, rubbing and circling it with his fingers.

The smell of sweat and sex grew more pronounced. Their breathing filled the little room with rasps and sighs and shattered moans. Fionn continued to move inside her, and Kieran continued to stroke over her increasingly wet folds, his fingers inching forward a little farther each time.

Suddenly, Fionn stiffened. His breath exploded from his lungs in a shattered gasp as his rhythm faltered to a heavy-breathing halt. His thigh muscles, pressed against Aine's legs and butt, were bunched hard as iron.

Aine's surprise lasted less than an instant. She had a pretty good idea what had happened. Kieran's questing fingers must have brushed against Fionn's cock. When Kieran stroked again, and Fionn jerked backward, out of reach, almost pulling out of her entirely in the process, she was sure of it.

"Don't," she groaned, not even certain to which of them she was speaking, but it was Kieran whose gaze she met. "Don't stop now." His eyes turned even darker as they stared at each other for a long, wordless moment; then his gaze swept past her to connect with Fionn's. Or so she assumed, for what else would he be looking at over her shoulder?

The uncertain, pleading expression in Kieran's eyes was Aine's undoing. "Please, Fionn," she begged again. "Don't stop."

Fionn's hand, still clenched on Aine's hip, trembled. He dropped his head to her shoulder and groaned in protest. "Aine."

"Please. I need this." *As do you, and he as well...*

They all needed this. She was more sure now than ever. They needed something unlike what she and Fionn had now, or what she and Kieran might someday have together.

Something they could only experience when all three of them were present. Not better perhaps, but different. Proof—for whoever was still uncertain—that they all needed each other, that she needed them both, that no one was in any danger of being left out.

Growling beneath his breath, Fionn adjusted his grip. He clasped her hips with both hands and pulled her to him, practically dragging her onto his cock. He resumed thrusting inside her, hard, fast, almost angrily.

Kieran's gaze was still fixed on Fionn's face, his eyes narrowed, his expression intent, yearning, hungry. His touch no longer teased; it demanded. He ground the heel of his palm against Aine's mound, letting the motion of Fionn's hips carry her forward, letting each hard thrust deliver her right into his hand. Kieran's thumb slid against Aine's clit with every stroke. Need spiraled out of control within her. She was certain the rest of Kieran's fingers were caressing Fionn's cock at the same time, circling him in almost the same way Aine's fingers encircled Kieran's.

It was that single thought, the realization that they were all touching each other so intimately, learning and pleasuring each other so completely, that catapulted her over the edge. She cried out as she came, the sound cut off as Kieran surged against her, capturing her mouth with his. Her hand tightened convulsively around his cock. And when he slid a finger inside her, forcing her sex to open wider, allowing Fionn's cock to touch her more deeply, causing her internal muscles to clamp down harder with each racking spasm, she came completely undone.

And the two men were right there with her. Keiran's finger was buried in her center, feeling each spasm, each clench, each pulse of her sex and giving Fionn exactly what he needed too: an extra bit of pressure alongside his shaft, as his woman writhed uncontrollably in his arms, sobbing his name with every breath.

Fionn stiffened once more. His hips snapped forward in short, sharp thrusts. Again. Again. Once again. His fingers dug into Aine's hip as he buried himself deep and spilled inside her.

As Aine struggled to catch her breath, Kieran gentled his touch. He slid his finger out of her body and shifted around until he could wrap his other hand around hers—the one that still clutched his dripping shaft. Still unable to move, Aine was content to watch as Kieran took up the rhythm she'd lost, using both their hands to stroke his cock.

The grip of Kieran's hand on hers, the thrust of his cock through her fingers, Fionn nuzzling her ear and neck and combing his fingers through her hair—it all felt so good. She never wanted it to end. But gradually Kieran's touch became more urgent, his breathing more erratic. Suddenly, it was not enough.

"Fionn," she whispered urgently. "Let me go a minute."

AT THE SOUND of his name, Fionn lifted his head and looked at Aine inquiringly. Then his gaze strayed. He glanced across at Kieran and couldn't look away. Something in Fionn's chest tightened and twisted at the sight of the man.

Kieran lay with his head thrown back, his eyes screwed shut, his hand in busy motion. It had been a long, long time since Fionn had seen Kieran look just so. A hot flush rose in Fionn's face. His balls tightened, and his cock, still lodged inside Aine, so recently sated, pulsed with a resurgence of need.

It was all he could do to keep himself from launching himself across her and throwing himself atop the other man. He wanted to wrap his hand around Kieran's cock and make the Holly King come for *him*, with *him*, under *him*...

"Fionn," Aine repeated, her voice faintly pleading.

Fionn dragged his gaze back to her face. It didn't take him but a moment to read the question in her eyes, to read the need there and understand what she wanted. She wanted Kieran, wanted to take his cock inside her like she'd just taken Fionn's. And how could he blame her for that when he wanted very much the same thing himself?

Still, his pulse started to race as he remembered the feel of Kieran's fingers on his shaft only a few moments earlier. Being touched by them both had made Fionn come harder than he ever had in his life. Pouring himself into Aine, knowing he was coating Kieran's fingers with his seed at the exact same time, nothing had ever felt more right, more perfect.

But it wasn't right—not now, not for him. And even that small taste of Kieran—so dangerous, so tempting, so impossible to deny—had been too much. All by itself it had taken Fionn to the very edge of surrender, far too close to that line he could not let himself cross, not ever again.

Perhaps, after all, it was better this way. Perhaps watching the two of them together would be enough to satisfy him, or to at least ease the craving. It was all he should wish for, the closest he could ever safely come to having what he really wanted.

Sighing reluctantly, Fionn leaned in and pressed a chaste kiss against his wife's cheek. Then he eased himself out of Aine's body. He moved back a little—but only as far as he could without breaking contact. He needed to touch her for as long as he could.

Aine pulled her hand free of Kieran's and then rolled onto her back. The Holly King's eyes slitted open. He gazed at her uncertainly. Aine reached for him. "Come here to me now," she said in a voice made thick and slow with lust—just the way Fionn liked it. From the way Kieran's eyes blazed with sudden heat, he liked it too.

Kieran's eyes cut quickly to Fionn's face. Too quickly. He gave Fionn no time at all to school his features into a neutral expression. Fionn didn't know what Kieran had seen there, but whatever it was must have reassured him, because he wasted no time, quickly settling himself between Aine's thighs, caging her in his arms, gazing down at her with a rapt expression that seemed to contain all the adoration Fionn also felt when he looked at her. All the adoration he remembered having once felt when he looked at Kieran as well in those days before other feelings, of guilt and regret and helpless fury, took its place.

"Beautiful Aine," Kieran murmured, between kisses. "Do you know how much I've wanted you, how often I've thought of having you like this over the past year?"

"I've wanted you too," Aine answered as she wrapped her legs around his hips and pulled him close.

Groaning softly, Kieran thrust into her, sheathing himself to the hilt in her sweetness and her warmth. Fionn found himself gritting his teeth as jealousy reared its head.

"Ah, how wonderful." Kieran sighed. "How good you feel, so warm and real."

Aine splayed her hands on Kieran's back as they began to move together. Her restless fingers played across Kieran's skin, learning his shape, mapping his increasingly slick contours, clearly delighting in the feel of him in her arms. Watching her, watching the blissful expression on her face, Fionn's heart ached. Jealousy gave way to confusion, to a longing so sharp it pierced his soul. His experience with Kieran had been so brief, so hurried. What he wouldn't have given to have had the luxury of touching him like that, to touch him as much as he wanted for as long as he wanted. What he wouldn't give to be the one bringing her to ecstasy right now—again and again in the few hours they had left. Or to be the one who would get to wake up beside her on the morrow.

Perhaps he'd sighed aloud, because Aine turned her head in his direction. Inquisitive eyes sought him out, and as their gazes locked, she reached for him. While one arm remained draped around Kieran, the other stretched toward Fionn. He couldn't resist taking hold of her hand. He brought it to his lips and kissed her knuckles. She gave a little tug, as though to urge him closer, but he pretended not to notice. He couldn't get any closer. He couldn't take that risk.

Instead, he looked away, allowing his gaze to sweep down the length of their bodies. Stars above, he didn't know which of them he wanted more or who he'd give his soul to trade places with at that moment. His fingers itched to smooth down the length of Kieran's back. His mouth watered for a taste of him, for a chance to press his lips against the small of Kieran's back, to drag his tongue down along the crease of his ass, to inhale his musk, to delve between his cheeks...

When at last Fionn let his gaze return to Aine's face, he found her blue eyes glowing with heat. As their eyes locked with one another, the blood rose in Aine's cheeks. It was as if her whole body was reacting to the thought of Fionn watching as Kieran fucked her. A smile curled Fionn's lips. Perhaps, after all, there was still something he could do for her.

He let go of her hand but continued to hold her gaze. He got out of bed and moved to stand beside her head. He smiled reassuringly when her eyes flickered in apprehension. Apprehension quickly turned to heat when Fionn began to stroke himself. Out of the corner of his eye, Fionn saw Kieran turn his head to watch him too, but Fionn kept his attention focused on Aine.

At first, it was mostly for show, to add to Aine's pleasure and—perhaps—to steal a little of her attention away from Kieran. Fionn's cock was too soft, too recently satisfied for anything else—or so he thought. But then Aine's tongue swiped over her parted lips, and he jerked in response, his balls tightening as though it were they receiving her tongue's attention. He was surprised when he felt himself growing longer, harder, when he found himself swelling once again with need.

"Feed it to her." Kieran's voice was husky and raw; Fionn shuddered at the mere sound of it.

"Go on," Kieran urged. He glanced down at Aine and smiled. "You'd like that, wouldn't you, lass?"

Aine's expression grew guarded. Her gaze moved between them, hooded, calculating. Finally she nodded. She licked her lips again and then smiled. She nodded in agreement, and Fionn's cock turned even harder.

As though in a dream, Fionn moved closer to the bed. He was mesmerized by Kieran's voice, by the hungry, curious gleam that lit up Aine's eyes. He moved close enough to slide one knee onto the bed, close enough for Aine's tongue to slip out and sweep, hot and wet, across his weeping glans. When she opened her mouth wider, Fionn pushed in even closer, groaning in pleasure when her lips tightened around him. He rocked slowly back and forth, watching his cock where it disappeared into Aine's mouth, a little more each time. *Yes. Just like that.* Heat thickened inside him. Then Fionn's gaze strayed to Kieran's face. He lay atop Aine, not moving, his predatory gaze firmly fastened…on Fionn's cock.

Fionn pulled back, scowling. "You bastard. Why don't you pay some attention to what you're doing?" King or not, if Kieran couldn't treat Aine right, if he either couldn't or wouldn't give her what she wanted or provide her with all the respect and attention she deserved, then he didn't deserve to have her. Fionn would not let Kieran spend another six months with her, if that were the case; no, nor even six minutes. She was too important. Fionn would find some way to keep Kieran away from her. He wouldn't let him behave toward her the way he'd once behaved toward Fionn. He would not let him break her heart.

Kieran's eyebrows rose. He stared at Fionn in silence, then glanced at Aine. But she was also watching Fionn, eyes wide, a look of dawning wonder on her face. Fionn turned his head away. Why should she look so surprised? Did she not know he'd move heaven and earth to please her? Did she not know she deserved nothing less—from whomever she allowed into her bed? Out of the corner of his eye, Fionn watched as Kieran took Aine's chin in his hand and turned her to face him.

"Are you all right, lass?" he asked as they gazed tenderly at each other—his expression questioning, hers curious. After a moment, a smile curved Aine's lips. She nodded. In response, Kieran lowered his head and kissed her, briefly, gently. When he pulled back, she wrapped her arms around his neck and drew him back down for another kiss—longer, deeper, harder, hotter.

Fionn gritted his teeth. He felt equal parts angry and aroused as he watched them—openly now, unable to glance away as the two of them began to move together once again. A flush spread across Aine's face, and Fionn's fist tightened on his cock again, stroking in time to Kieran's thrusts, imagining himself in Kieran's place, making love to his wife; and also imagining that he was in Aine's place, lying beneath Kieran, staring up into his handsome face, taking him inside his body, meeting each thrust as best he could with his heels locked around Kieran's back. And feeling his heart and soul surrender to him.

Aine's breath grew choppy. When Kieran dropped his head to her shoulder and nipped the muscle there, she came hard. Throwing her head back, she keened loudly, and that sent Kieran off as well.

"Aine. Oh, my soul," Kieran groaned. He clutched her to him, breathing hard. They held each other tight, and Fionn, his hand falling still, could only watch. His heart pounded heavy and flat—dull as an old bodhran as understanding dawned within his heart. They already loved each other. He could read it in the twining of their limbs, the clasp of their hands, each tender gaze.

He stood there for a long moment, struggling to come to terms with his own unhappiness. Until, suddenly, Kieran surged off the bed and advanced upon him. Fionn fell back a step, his eyes narrowing. "Here now, what are you doing?" he demanded when Kieran stretched out a hand to him. "Stop right where you are."

The two men faced each other, Fionn scowling, Kieran…well, Fionn was not altogether certain what to think of the strained expression on Kieran's face, the dark intensity in his gaze.

"Will you not come back to bed?" Kieran asked at last. "Will you not give me leave to express my gratitude to you?"

Gratitude? Fionn shook his head. "Nay. That I'll not." Gratitude was the last thing he wanted from Kieran. Or the next to last, he supposed. To be given Kieran's pity would be even worse.

He was distantly aware that Aine had sat up and was watching the two of them from the bed. "Fionn, stop," she begged softly. "Please. Do not be so hard. It doesn't have to be like this."

"I know not what other way it can be," Fionn replied, his shoulders sagging. He wasn't sure yet what "this" was, never mind how it could be any different. He understood only that he was failing *her* expectations now too. A cold wind seemed to fill his soul. "My time here is nearly ended. I should go."

"No!" The anguished note in Aine's voice had both men flinching. "No. You can't. Not like this."

"This is my fault," Kieran murmured sadly. "I was wrong to agree to this."

"Aye, that you were," Fionn agreed. "You should not have come here. Not this year, nor last year either. You'd no business interfering in what did not concern you."

"Do you wish me to leave?" Kieran cast a wistful gaze toward the bed where Aine sat, still watching them, then turned back to Fionn. "To promise you that I'll stay away? Is that what you're asking?"

Was he? Fionn drew in a shaky breath. Could it really be that easy?

"Fionn, no," Aine protested again. "Don't."

Fionn rounded on her. "Is this what you want, then? Have you made your decision? You want him instead of me?"

"N-no." Aine gazed pleadingly at him, at both of them. "No, of course not. Not...not *instead*." She hung her head and added, "I'm sorry. I love you both."

"Maybe I *was* wrong to come here," Kieran said quietly, not looking at either of them. "Though in my heart I do not believe that to be so. And I cannot regret it, even if it is wrong. Even if you were to ask me to stay away from her now...I am not certain that I could." He raised his gaze to Fionn's face. "But that is not my main regret."

"Then what?"

Kieran met his gaze for a moment without speaking. A frisson of nerves raced up Fionn's spine as he took in the somber expression on Kieran's face. "I am sorry for the way I treated you—those many years ago, when first we met. As though you didn't matter. As though you were of no importance."

"I *wasn't* important. I was no one at all back then." And he'd give almost anything to be able to say that about himself now. How much simpler his life had been.

Kieran shook his head slowly. "Oh, but you're wrong. You were *always* important. And I was a fool for not seeing that fact more clearly. Why else would I have had to push you away so hard? You mattered so much more than I'd planned. More than I wanted. More than I had any idea what to do with." A sad smile curved his lips. "And that 'twas not the only time I've let you down, I fear. When you first became king...there was so much assistance I could have given you—that I *should* have given you and, indeed, that I *would* have done, had I not been so mired in my own grief. I might have made your path easier, your burden lighter—as was done for me."

It should have warmed Fionn's heart to hear Kieran speak like this, but it only made things worse. It made the loss he was feeling that much greater. And as for the unbearable gaps—between who he needed to be, who he wanted to be, and who he really was—those seemed to stretch wider than ever before. When Kieran took another hesitant step toward him, Fionn balled his hands into fists and snarled at him, "Stop."

Kieran paused. The look on his face was bleak, hopeless, resigned. "Is there naught I can do, then, to change your mind and win your forgiveness? Will you give me no hope at all?"

Fionn shook his head. "Why should I believe you now? Why should I listen to a word you say when I know you'd say anything at all just to win your point?"

"Fionn." The pain and sympathy in Aine's voice wrung Fionn's heart. "Please, my love. I believe him to be sincere. Can you not find it in you to give him a chance?"

He gazed at her in anguish. "You do not know what it is you're asking—or what he's asking. He's asking for a return to a time that is no more. I'm no longer so callow as once I was. I held my honor cheaply then and was easily persuaded by honeyed words. But even if I wanted to delude myself again, to lose myself in blissful ignorance, I cannot do so. I am the Oak King now, and I *will not* bring dishonor to the title." It was all he had, after all. He turned his gaze back on Kieran. "Do not ask me again for you, of all people, should know I cannot behave so." How many seasons of his youth had he wasted in just such a fashion, loitering about in the woods near to Kieran's tree, hoping to entice him, grateful for any attention—a look, a smile—aching to be used by him.

If they didn't stop right now, he'd be making a liar of himself by doing so again. "I cannot bend. I cannot humble myself. I cannot beg."

Kieran's eyes met his for an instant longer; his gaze piercing, his mouth stern. "I can." Then he dropped to his knees. He bowed his head and murmured humbly, "Please, my liege. I'm begging you."

Fionn's innards felt like they'd twisted into knots. "Get up off your knees and stop this foolishness. At once. 'Tis weakness, I tell you. 'Tis shameful. It becomes you not."

"No." Aine got out of bed and came to stand beside him. "'Tis neither weakness nor shame. 'Tis never that. I've listened to you both talk of what it means to be king, the service it entails, the giving of yourself, the sacrifice. It takes strength to willingly surrender oneself in such a manner. This is no different. It takes courage to allow yourself to be vulnerable, to give your heart into another's keeping. It takes love and courage and trust. And love... Oh, Fionn. Do you not see? That's the very thing that makes everyone equal."

"I would never think you weak," Kieran said as he gazed up at Fionn. "Never. Indeed, I know you to be far braver than I am. You followed your heart when you came here last year. You risked yourself for love. And that is something I've been afraid to do for far too long. Will you not be brave again tonight? Will you not follow your heart once more…for my heart's sake?"

Chapter Thirteen

A hush filled the room. Kieran's heart pounded. He felt grateful and terrified and shocked by his own boldness in asking Fionn to love him. Had he ever risked so much on so slight a chance? Had he ever tempted fate so recklessly? He'd received so much tonight. How dare he even hope for more?

Fionn stared back at him, his expression blank. Kieran had no idea what he was feeling, no idea if there was any hope his pleas would be heard. He had done all he could, however. Now all that was left was to wait—for who knew how long. Perhaps it would take years, perhaps decades, perhaps centuries.

Or perhaps…it would take no time at all.

Fionn moved suddenly. Kieran found himself being hauled to his feet and then pulled into Fionn's arms. Their teeth clashed, lips splitting at the impact as their mouths met in a harsh and violent kiss. Kieran sucked in a quick and startled breath. Before he could fully process what was happening, Fionn pulled back to stare at him. His eyes blazed with heat as they met Kieran's. With heat, with need, with heartbreaking uncertainty.

Kieran's own heart ached. He reached out tentatively and took hold of Fionn's hip. He urged him close with gentle pressure. Their second kiss was more restrained but no less passionate. Kieran's head reeled as the taste, the smell, the feel of Fionn saturated all his senses. His arms slid around the Oak King's back, molding the two of them closer together. Their erections brushed against one another— impossible to tell who was harder, more desperate, more ready.

Kieran broke the kiss with a groan. Dipping his head, he nipped at Fionn's neck, eliciting an answering groan. His arms shook. Much as he wanted to slip a hand between their bodies and clasp Fionn's cock—or no, better yet, to clasp both their cocks together, to stroke and squeeze—his arms refused his orders. He could not relax his grasp or release Fionn for even a minute.

Suddenly, they were in motion again. Kieran nearly lost his footing as he felt himself propelled backward several steps until his legs smacked against the edge of the bed. He went down hard, landing on his back, with Fionn on top of him.

Kieran stared up at Fionn, even more breathless than before. Here was joy and passion and everything he had missed for far too long. He felt as though a fire had been relit in the darkness of his soul.

"Want you," Fionn muttered, brushing rough kisses against Kieran's neck and shoulder. "Now. Need to feel your cock inside me once again tonight. Just once before I go."

A shudder worked its way down Kieran's spine. "Aye." He nodded agreement, regretting the need for haste, all the time he'd wasted, all his fear and indecision. "I should have come here sooner. We could have had more time that way." Or maybe he should have *said* something sooner—years ago, decades. Maybe it would have made a difference, maybe they would not be rushing now. Or maybe everything had to happen in its proper time and in its proper season.

Aine's face appeared, hovering behind Fionn's shoulder, and Kieran knew he was right about that, for here was his proof. Without her, they might never have had this. He might never have found the courage to speak, never been spurred into action, never opened his eyes to what he was missing. It was possible he and Fionn could have eventually been able to move past the mistakes in their past without her. But what if they could not?

In fact, without those mistakes, without every misstep they'd each taken, he and Fionn might have never met Aine, never found their way here, never have had this…and maybe this was what they were all meant to have had from the start. It was a paradox, to be sure, and those were best chalked up to fate and destiny and written off as incomprehensible. Not even several centuries would suffice to puzzle out the answers to some questions.

"Let me up." Kieran pushed at Fionn's chest. "Change places with me. I want you on your back this time." An eager flush colored Fionn's face, but still he hesitated. His eyes grew dark with uncertainty. For a moment, Kieran wondered if he meant to refuse. "Please," he added. "I want to look into your eyes. I want to watch your face as I join with you."

Fionn swallowed hard. He dropped his gaze, apparently unable to look at either of them as he got to his feet.

Smiling in anticipation, Kieran turned to Aine. "Lass, have you any sort of oil about? Even butter would do in a pinch." He could improvise, of course, if he had to. Certainly both he and Fionn had done without any such thing upon occasion in the past, but he'd rather not do so tonight. It was too important, and it had been too long for both of them. "We just need something with which to slick our way."

Color flared on Aine's face. "I'll go and see."

She slipped from bed and scampered quickly from the room. Fionn turned to watch her go, his expression uncertain once again.

Kieran cleared his throat to get Fionn's attention. "And now, my liege, if you'd be so kind." He bowed politely. "Would you oblige me by lying down here, right here on the edge, with your legs hanging over the bed?"

A small frown formed on Fionn's brow. He shook his head. "No titles tonight," he corrected. He pulled Kieran into his arms for a quick embrace, then pressed another feverish kiss against his lips. "Tonight I'm just Fionn."

"As you wish. And I will be just Kieran, then."

Fionn snorted. "As if you could. I don't believe there's such a thing as *just* Kieran. You've far too many facets."

Kieran laughed in response. "I like the sound of that. And I rather hope you're correct. But the same might also be said of you."

Fionn shook his head. "Not tonight."

By the time Aine returned, Kieran had Fionn in

position, just where he wanted him. He himself was crouched on the floor beside the bed, already at work between Fionn's legs, stretching and opening him, getting him ready to take his cock.

A hot flush colored Aine's face as her gaze took in the sight of the two men. Kieran sat back on his heels and took the small bottle of herbed oil she offered him. When he uncapped it, all the varied scents of a summer's day seemed to fill the room. He breathed deeply and smiled as memories flooded his mind. "Ah, thank you. This is perfect."

While Kieran busied himself with the oil, Aine climbed back into bed. She leaned over Fionn and pressed her lips to the head of her husband's shaft. His shattered groan was all the encouragement she needed, apparently, for she was soon happily employed licking and sucking him, running her tongue around his cock's thick rim—arousing him all over again, distracting him from the burn when Kieran too hastily pressed his oil-slicked fingers inside, driven by the lustful need that had a fire racing through his veins.

Not that Fionn seemed to care. "Oh, so good," he moaned as he threw back his head and gave himself over to their ministrations.

Still, Kieran forced himself to slow down. Shifting lower, he applied his lips and tongue to the task as well, tugging at Fionn's sac, delving between his cheeks, teasing and stabbing and circling the softening flesh. Glancing up, his gaze met Aine's. His rhythm faltered, as did hers. It was hard to decide which sight affected him more, that of her lips stretched wide around Fionn's girth, or that look in her eyes, the heat that darkened them.

"Ah, don't stop." Fionn moaned again. "More. Give me more." And Kieran bent himself once more to the task, rubbing circles with his thumbs, fluttering his tongue over Fionn's most sensitive flesh, curving and twisting his digits within Fionn's channel until Fionn's moans turned to shouts of pleasure and his legs shook with the effort to hold himself back.

Finally, however, Kieran could take no more. His own body was demanding a share of his attention. His cock was painfully hard, already dripping, throbbing with need. He pulled his fingers free of Fionn's body. "I'm sorry," he said as he straightened up once more. "I can wait no longer."

Aine released Fionn's cock and reluctantly made to back away, but Kieran stopped her. "No. You're a part of this too now, lass. Come. Sit astride him. I want him to feel us both at once."

"Oh, ye gods," Fionn groaned, eyes shuttering closed. He covered his face with his hands and swallowed hard yet again.

Aine's gaze flickered back and forth between the two men. "Fionn?" she asked uncertainly. "Are you all right, my love? Is this truly what you want?"

Fionn dropped his hands and opened his eyes again. He met her gaze, his eyes blazing with heat. "Oh, Aine. Aye. I never dreamed of such a thing, to have you both at once, but never doubt it's what I want. Indeed, I'm beginning to suspect the two of you know my heart's desires better than I do myself."

Aine's face relaxed. She was smiling wickedly as she swung one leg over Fionn's midsection. Kieran placed one hand on her hip to steady her. With his other hand, he found Fionn's shaft and guided it to Aine's opening. Aine lowered herself onto Fionn, slowly seating herself. All three groaned in concert.

Kieran rose to his feet. He shifted closer and then wrapped his hands around the backs of Fionn's thighs and pressed them open. "'Twill have to be fast, I'm afraid," he said, regretfully, grimacing a little as he gazed down at Fionn. "Seeing you like this is almost enough to set me off, all on its own. I'm not going to last."

Fionn smiled crookedly back at him. "No, and no more will I."

"I doubt any of us will," Aine agreed, already breathless.

"It's too long I've been wanting this," Kieran said as he fitted himself to Fionn's opening. He pushed in slowly, slowly, slowly. Then pulled out and slammed back in again. "It's been far too long."

FIONN GROANED AS the pressure built and his cock lengthened and swelled, as he felt himself surrounded by his lovers. Their movements shifted in and out of rhythm with each other, and the resultant chaos only heightened his sensations. Indeed, Fionn's senses were so severely overloaded with pleasure he could scarcely breathe. It was so good, so very good. His only complaint was the speed at which they were pushing him toward climax when he wanted to prolong the experience indefinitely. His first time with Kieran had been just this fast. Now they were rushing once again, racing for the finish when they ought to be savoring every moment.

All too soon they were coming apart. Aine cried out softly. Fionn pulled her down onto his chest and kissed her deeply while her body shook and contracted all around him. Then it was his turn. Fionn's gaze sought Kieran's over Aine's shoulder as his breath caught and his body gave way. He climaxed impaled on Kieran's cock and drowning in the other man's eyes while Aine held him close and pressed kisses to his chest and throat. And, finally, Kieran joined them. The hands that held Fionn's legs shook as Kieran stiffened suddenly. Groaning loudly, he gave one last thrust and buried himself as deep as he could in Fionn's body.

Fionn was still struggling to catch his breath when Kieran slumped forward. He rested his head against Aine's back, then pressed a kiss against her shoulder blade. She moaned so contentedly that breathless though he was, Fionn could scarcely keep from laughing. Gone was the doubt that had all but consumed his mind. He felt light, joyful, reborn.

After shifting Aine to one side of him, Fionn reached for Kieran and dragged him onto the bed as well until they had all collapsed in an exhausted heap. Fionn sighed happily.

It had all been so perfect. He was almost shocked to find that there was still one small complaint lodged deep within in his mind. It had been over too soon.

It hardly mattered, however. Indeed, it was barely a ripple on the surface of the deep well of his peace. Because next time—ah, next time—by all the stars that spangled the sky overhead, Fionn vowed they'd be taking this much more slowly.

* * * *

"It's time." The sound of Kieran's voice, quiet and so ineffably sad, shook Aine awake. A shiver of apprehension raced over her nerves. Something was happening. "I've done what I could, but dawn will not be held back forever."

Fionn sighed in response, breathy and soft, like a summer breeze rattling the leaves. "I know."

Aine sat up. She scanned the still-dark room until her gaze finally located the two men, limned in moonlight as they stood facing each other in front of the bedroom window. As she watched, the two figures moved closer, merging with one another until they were locked in a passionate embrace. She watched as they kissed, as the kiss deepened, lingered, as the two men clung ever more tightly to one another. A long, long moment passed; then another gusty sigh filled the air. The two men broke away from one another.

"Fionn?" Her voice broke the silence, sounding too loud and far too shaky. Fionn turned his head. "What's happening?" she asked, even though she knew the answer. From the moon's angle, it was clear the time was well after midnight.

"I'm afraid I must be going now, a grádh." Fionn crossed the room and knelt by the bed. "The night is ending; day will soon be here."

"No." Tears sparked in Aine's eyes. "Not yet." She threw herself into his arms and held on tight. When his lips found hers, she kissed him back with all the passion she possessed. Why could not her love for him hold back this parting just a little longer? Why could he not stay by her side for just a few hours more? But even as she thought it, she knew it was a forlorn hope. Whether fast or slow the time for their parting must eventually arrive and be just as grievous.

"I'm sorry," Fionn whispered against her lips. "I have to go."

Aine nodded. "I know." Blinking back her tears, she pulled away from him and forced a smile. "And after all, what's a few short months?"

Fionn reached for her hand and lifted it to his lips. He pressed a soft kiss against her knuckles. "Without you, it will seem an eternity."

Aine shook her head. "But you will not be without me. Never think it. I'll be right here awaiting your return. Always."

"Aine. My love." Fionn kissed her hand again, one last time. Then he let her go. Smiling sadly, he climbed to his feet.

Just like last year, he managed to take only a few steps away from her when, once again, the wind took him, spinning him around like a top and sweeping him from her sight. Aine cried out in dismay and ran to the window, thinking there must be some sign of him, some way to tell which way he went. But the night was silver and black, with nary a breeze. She blinked in surprise. "He's gone."

"Nay, never think it." Kieran wrapped his arms around her from behind and rested his chin on her head. "'Tis as close as yon woods, he is—no farther. Only a short walk away, and for just a little while at that. He'll be back again to gladden our hearts practically before we know it."

Aine leaned back against him and sighed. "I know."

"And you'll still have me in the meantime. That has to be worth something, I hope?"

Aine turned in his arms. A twisted smile graced his lips. "I think you mean we still have each other," she said, as she laid a palm against his cheek. "And I would say that it's worth a great deal."

"That it is." Kieran captured her hand and brought it to his lips, kissing her just as Fionn had done and in exactly the same place. "That it is, my love. Always."

Chapter Fourteen

The world was not what it once was. Of that Fionn O'Dair was certain. It was a bright and beautiful place this pristine morning. A world reborn. Though it still slumbered in its snowy bed, he could feel the life within it. Curled up and folded in upon itself, like a seed in the dark, it awaited the light of the sun's rays to quicken it and bring it forth. As his mind expanded outward, Fionn was aware of the joy that lay at the center of all creation. He could feel it aching to break free and explode into the world in swollen creeks after a spring thaw, in sweet-scented blossoms unfurling on a leafy branch, in newborn lambs dancing in the meadow.

He felt like dancing himself, if only that were possible. It was not, however. It would be several long months before he could dance again. But this morning, even that was all right. He was content to stand here, tall and proud, ruling over the woodlands, protecting all that he held dear.

Their voices carried on the clear morning air. The sound reached him long before they came into view. He was grateful that his thoughts had not yet been wholly absorbed by the Forestmind, that it was not yet too late for him to hear them. He felt a thrill of longing, of recognition, of love. Aine. And Kieran. Coming out to say good-bye.

Fionn watched their approach. His wife looked glorious this morning. Her hair was all the colors of sunrise, and the long green cloak she wore, while it concealed more than he would have liked, was the perfect color for someone espoused to the Greenworld. Kieran, meanwhile, looked his dashing, regal self, a fitting consort for her. A fitting consort for *me* as well, Fionn thought with no small amount of pride.

Finally, they reached the base of Fionn's tree. "We bid you a good morning, sire," Kieran said as he laid a hand flat against Fionn's bark. "And wish you well as your reign begins."

Fionn felt a faint trace of warmth at the point of contact, one that deepened and spread until his heart was filled with love and contentment.

"Be at peace, beloved," Kieran murmured, his voice dark and low, rough with emotion. "And never fear. For I shall take good care of your lady in your absence."

Our lady, Fionn corrected silently; and take care of yourself as well. Already his mind had turned to thoughts of summer, when the world would once more be green and alive. The scant few hours he and Kieran would have to spend together then would not be nearly enough time for all Fionn wanted to do. Most of it would have to wait until next winter. He knew he could trust his magician of the 'Tween to contrive to stretch time to its fullest then—and all for their benefit.

Aine spread her arms wide and pressed herself against Fionn's trunk. "Rule well, my love," she whispered. How Fionn wished he had arms to embrace her back. There was no breeze to shake his branches, yet shake they did, raining down a drift of crystal kisses to gently brush her upturned face. Aine laughed in delight as she gazed up at him adoringly, but Fionn caught a hint of tears sparkling in her blue eyes.

Aine's lips were trembling as she took a step back. Kieran wrapped his arms around her, as Fionn could not. The words he spoke were too quiet for Fionn to hear, but Aine nodded in response and snuggled closer. Kieran bent and pressed a kiss upon her cheek.

Once upon a time, Fionn thought dreamily as his mind continued to spin away, the thought of the two of them comforting each other like this in his absence would have driven him mad, would have filled him with rage and resentment. Once…was it only yesterday? Now, the thought brought him peace and contentment. He was glad they had each other and that he had them both. That none of them need ever feel alone again. Ah, what a difference one day could make. What a difference love could make.

"He'll likely outlive us both, won't he?" Aine asked in a voice that trembled slightly.

Kieran hesitated. "As to that, I cannot say. For who am I to know what the future may hold? I thought the same of Rory, and you see how that turned out. On the other hand, it is equally possible that the same magic that sustains us might extend your life as well."

"But in the normal way of things?"

His face grave, Kieran nodded. "Yes, it is most likely we shall both predecease him. Why? Does that trouble you?"

Aine shook her head. "I have outlived one husband already. It is enough, I think. But…does he know that?"

"I imagine he does. It's likely he'd have thought of it."

"He is very brave, isn't he?"

"He is, indeed." Kieran looked at her curiously. "But what is it prompts you to say so now?"

"Why, the way he loves us. And that he should continue to do so, even knowing the pain we'll likely cause him when we go."

"Of course." Kieran sighed gustily. "You are right again, my love." He tightened his arms and pulled her even closer. "He is indeed the best and bravest of us all."

For a moment longer, the three of them stood there, Aine and Kieran huddled companionably beneath Fionn's branches. All the while the Oak King's thoughts drifted and spread, traveling throughout the forests and the woodlands, all across the Greenworld; life calling to life. Far and wide his thoughts went, to the ends of the earth and back again, whispering the world awake on this perfect winter morning.

About PG Forte

PG Forte inhabits a world only slightly less strange than the ones she creates. Filled with serendipity, coincidence, love at first sight, and dreams come true, it also bears an uncanny resemblance to Berkeley, California.

She wrote her first serialized story when she was still in her teens. The sexy, ongoing adventure tales were very popular at her oh-so-proper, all girls, Catholic High School, where they helped to liven up otherwise dull classes…even if her teachers didn't always think so.

Originally a Jersey girl, PG now resides with her family on the extreme left coast where she writes rule bending, genre blending contemporary romance and paranormal stories. It's a tough job, but someone's got to do it.

Links to reach PG Forte:

www.PGForte.com
Facebook.com/AuthorPGForte
Twitter.com/PGForte

www.ingramcontent.com/pod-product-compliance
Lightning Source LLC
Chambersburg PA
CBHW071343170626
46811CB00003B/965